# THE NAUGHTY LIST

## Book One of Elijah Joseph

## The Wolfe Legacy

## J. R. Froemling

This is a work of fiction.

Names, characters, places, and incidents are used fictitiously.

Any resemblance to actual events, locales, or persons, living or dead, is entirely coincidental.

This one is definitely for my husband!
He inspires me to write every day.
He supports me when I do not feel strong.
He is my world and my everything.
I love you, Ben.

# The Wolfe Legacy

## Hope-Marie Wolfe

- Mistress Giselle (1978-1983)

## Elijah Joseph Wolfe

- The Naughty List (1986)

# CHAPTER ONE
## *Season's Greetings*

"Wolfe! Get your ass in here." I had just settled in to read the latest cold case when the portly man across the office bellowed for my attention. I cock an eyebrow and steal a glance at the tempting pastry on my desk. Do I have enough time to enjoy breakfast? No, I decide. I pick up my coffee in resignation, and trudge into the captain's office.

"Sir?"

"Close the door and take a seat." He then plops down with a grunt.

I comply without issue. It's early, and the captain is always a grouch before his coffee. I hold my cup of coffee in my hand as he stares at me. Nothing good comes from him being quiet. I begin ticking through all the reasons he could be pissed right now. I hadn't touched that beat cop in at least a week. No incidents in the gym. Kept to myself at my desk. I even held the door for that blow-hard in booking yesterday.

"Damn Feds want to horn in on the Santa case."

"You mean the one where the rent-a-Santas are gettin' jumped for their red buckets?" I lean forward. I had heard

Hatchett and Cleaver talking about the case. Damn idiots were only half-ass interviewing the Santas and had gotten nowhere.

"Yeah. That's the one. Seems like the idiot doing it decided to jump the river. Now it's a 'federal interstate crime spree'," he barks at me, complete with hand waves and eye roll. "So, you know what I say? The feds want it? They can have it. Lets me put my boys back on real cases."

"What's that got to do with me, sir?"

"I'll tell you what it's got to do with you. You," he points at me and smirks, "just got babysitting duty."

"Babysitting duty?"

"Did I stutter, Wolfe? They are bringing some greenhorn that needs their hand held for investigating in Kansas City. So that's where you come in. It's a nice, easy, do-nothing job." He then starts bullet-pointing on his fingers. "That means no assaults. No complaints. No destruction of property. No illegal searches without warrants. No bullying. And most of all, Wolfe, no deaths."

"Okay, sir." I didn't think my days as a beat cop were so violent to warrant this level of restrictions to my work. I chuckle at the captain.

"Don't you laugh at this. This is serious, Wolfe. I saw how your uncle worked, and you are a chip off the old block. You keep your nose straight, and we're good."

"Awoo," I bark as if I had just said Hoo-Ah. This wins me a dark look from the captain. I am sure he was about to grind my gears when the door opens and in walked trouble with a capital T. As my pop always says that rhymes with P and stands for pool. Yah, I know it's from The Music Man. But it applies and I would shoot that any day of the week. She is a hot little brunette wearing slacks, a white dress shirt, and suit jacket. Her heals tick like a bomb about to go off as she makes her way to the desk. By the time my gaze trails up to her face, she is staring daggers at me. I cough a little and stand like Maman told me to do whenever a lady enters the room, albeit a little late. I was busy taking in the scenery.

"Where's Harris, Frank? You said you'd bring your agent." I hear the captain grumble behind me.

I caught the dark look behind her eyes before she smothered it with a dazzling smile. "Hi. I'm Agent Harris. Pleasure to meet you." I hear Trouble say as she offers a hand to shake with the captain.

"You robbin' nunneries now, Frank?" The captain shakes her hand briefly before motioning for them to sit.

"Charlie, she's a damn good agent. Graduated top of her class. So, tell me about this liaison you have picked out for me. I hear he's a real horn dog," Frank says with a devious grin on his face. It is hard to not laugh out loud at the two men measuring their dicks in this room.

The captain snorts and cuts me a severe look as if to say he is adding 'No fucking.' to the laundry list of don'ts for this case. I reach out a hand to offer Agent Harris, "Joe Wolfe."

She looks at my hand, then draws her gaze up to mine. There is that little dark look flashing in her eyes before she grasps my hand roughly to shake. "The pleasure is all yours, I'm sure."

"Well, I mean, if you like me to share my pleasure…" I flash her my best Wolfe grin.

Frank and captain share a look before they turn to stare at me. She retracts her hand and turns to face Frank, "I told you. I don't need a babysitter. I got this. Why not let him go chase some meter maid's skirt while we work?"

See, Trouble.

I sit back down in my chair and cock an eyebrow to the captain, who is grinning like a fox in the henhouse. I'm interested in seeing where this goes from here.

"Well, missy. Since you haven't been on the case, you don't know all the history. And Wolfe here, is probably the best at gettin' you acclimated to how we do things in Kansas City."

I know this to be complete and utter bullshit, as Hatchett and Cleaver were the ones in charge of this case. This asshole didn't think I was detective material. Good to know.

"Listen, *captain*," I hear Trouble say as she draws out his title as an insult. "I'm sure you boys think you know how to run this show, but this is a federal case. We're just letting you play along so you might learn something other than chest bumping and howling your awoos to the moon." I cannot help but grin at the balls on this woman.

"Harris. That's enough." Frank points to both of us, "You two are now partners. It is a joint effort to get it solved quickly. We can't have people afraid on Christmas. I expect this case to be wrapped up nice and tight before I head home for the holidays."

Trouble rolls her eyes, but nods. I nod as well. "Yes, sir."

"Great. Where are the files?" Agent Harris snipes at the room as she stands. I stand with her and motion with my head. I can't help but grin as I lead her across the bullpen to where Hatchett and Cleaver sit. I take immense pleasure in rifling through the stack of papers on their desks for the files I need.

"Hey! Get your hands off my shit, Wolfe," Cleaver says with a menacing tone.

"Cap'n said I'm on this case," I waggle the file at him as I back away. "Merry Christmas! You can go back to your doughnuts and beer."

When I finally turn, Trouble is standing there with a pole-axed look on her face. That alone makes this little scene all worth it.

"Wait. You weren't even on this case?" Anger flashes across her pretty face, and I get a weird sense of déjà vu.

"I am now," as I lead her back to my humble abode in the far corner of the bullpen.

"Please tell me you are at least a detective," she grumbles.

"Yup! Earned my badge last month," I smirk.

"Of course, you did," she says. She then looks around for a place to sit down other than the perp chair and sighs when it is the only one available. I find it adorable how she sulks in the chair, but her interest is piqued, and her temper gone as I read aloud the details of the case. It only takes about twenty minutes to read through all the files we have and go over the statements we have gotten. As we are talking, I get the strange feeling I should know her. The pert little nose, cute pouty lips, and the way she keeps giving me side-eye suggests I have, in fact, fucked her. There goes that rule. I would remember had we had sex. She's too hot to forget. She isn't my usual. But I'd unwrap that present if I found it under the tree.

"Would you pay attention, Wolfe?" Her voice is full of irritation as she snaps her fingers in front of my face.

"Here I thought I was paying attention," I grin.

"My tits have nothing to do with this case, eyes up, mister." She motions up to her face from her tits.

"Yes, ma'am," I say with my charming drawl. I notice a sweet blush on her cheeks as I take my time staring into her eyes.

About that time, I get beaned in the head with a wad of paper, forcing me to tear away the smolder from Trouble to see the culprit of my assault.

"Stop seducing the new girl, Wolfe." I hear Peters whine from his desk. "Some of us have to remember we are *happily* married, after all. Quit showin' off and do your job."

By the time my eyes get back to Trouble, the most delicious blush has blossomed into a righteous fury blazing on her face. Holy terror is about to befall my head.

"Rest assured, *detective*, if Joe Wolfe were the last man on Earth, we would be extinct."

"Oh! Burn! Shot down in flames," Peters laughs. This draws the rest of the bullpen into jovial shaming of me and my failed attempt at seduction. Agent Harris is not amused. While we're laughing and jabbing each other, she snatches the file and storms out. It's then I noticed my beloved pastry is gone as well. That I cannot let stand. I snatch my gun out of the drawer, grab the jacket off the back of my chair, and give chase.

## CHAPTER TWO

### *On The First Day of Christmas*

I came out the door in a rush and there she was, leaning against my 1973 bright red Pontiac Firebird, with the onyx bird sprawling across the hood. I had worked the entire summer of 1975 to save up for that car and it's my baby.

My baby that she is touching.

I narrow my eyes at her as she licks her fingers to erase the evidence of her first crime today.

"That was my breakfast," I grumble at her.

"I don't know what you're talking about, Wolfe." She has a glint in her eyes as she smiles at me. "I thought you and your ego were being fed enough by your adoring fans in the bullpen."

"Ha. Ha. Figured out where we're going yet?" I move closer to shoo her off my baby. I run my hand along the car where her ass was touching it. I see her roll her eyes.

"No. I have a map. Was going to take the notes, if you can call them that, and mark all the instances where Santa has been attacked."

"Perfect! That means we have time for breakfast. I'm

driving," as I head toward the plain brown Ford LTD Crown Victoria on the other side of the parking lot.

"Wait! What about your Firebird?" She comes trotting up next to me.

"I'm not taking my bright red Firebird on a stakeout. Now, if you wanna go on a date later, sure. I might even let you take the stick," I say as I wink at her.

"Pig," she mutters as she rolls her eyes. "I am not going on a date with you. Not now. Not ever, Wolfe."

"Well, then I guess you're never gonna see how my stick handles." I shrug as I duck into the driver's seat.

"I already know how you handle your stick," she says with a smug look as she slides into the passenger seat. I shake my head as I drive off. A few minutes later we are pulling into a small diner near the station. The little bell chimes on the door as we step in, and we take up residence in a booth.

"What can I get ya, Wolfe?" The cute waitress is talking to me but looking at Trouble with a questioning look.

"I'll take the usual," I say as I smile at Connie. She's cute, but her father would shoot me.

"I'll have coffee and toast with jelly," Trouble offers. Then the waitress is gone. I watch in amusement as Agent Harris meticulously pulls out her map and unfurls it on the table. This is followed by the sorry excuse of a case file, and a pen. She never once looks up at me or asks me a question. She ticks down the list marking the locations on the map. I had already put together the basic area of where we needed to focus, but due diligence is never a bad thing. Shows she gives a damn about this petty case. I can't help but wonder whose Wheaties she pissed in to get assigned to this. About the time she marks the last of the locations on the map, the waitress comes back and sets down what can only be described as a 'heart attack on a plate'.

"What is that?"

"This, my dear Agent Harris, is the ultimate breakfast. Two biscuits, sausage patties, with bacon, scrambled eggs, and all of it buried under a divine amount of gravy."

"I see," she says with disdain.

"It's delicious. Want some?"

"I'll just have the toast," she picks up the little jelly packet and cracks it open to spread on her pitiful triangles of bread.

"Suit yourself," I shrug as I shove a hearty bite into my mouth.

"Hmph." She makes that little hum noise women make that drives me crazy. She obviously wants to say something, but she makes that sound instead and now I'm chasing my dick around trying to figure out what I did wrong. I ignore her while I enjoy my breakfast, and she seems content enough to ignore me. She buries her nose back into the case notes and reads through the various encounters as she narrows down where she wants to stake out. I take the silent moments to take her in. She is a looker, that's for sure. Enough of one that I am contemplating if the consequences of breaking the captain's rules would be worth it.

I shove another bite in and I *know* I know her from somewhere. I close one eye and cock my head to see if it gives me a clue.

"It's rude to stare," she says without looking up at me.

"Also, rude to steal someone's breakfast."

"Got any proof I stole it?" She looks up and smirks at me.

"Guess I'll have to frisk you to see if you stashed any of the evidence."

"I would like to see you try, Wolfe."

"Is that a bet, a threat, or a promise?" I flash her a wolfish grin.

"Guess you'll just have to find out." This saucy little minx grins and pops a piece of toast in her mouth like she had won this verbal tête-à-tête.

"So, promise. Good to know. Figured out we're going to be staking out Sears, yet?"

"How did you-?" she asks with an astonished look on her face.

"I mean, not that hard. They were all clustered in that area." I motion with my fork. "Sears is the one that makes the most sense." I had already built the map mentally, as the addresses had been read off at the bullpen. I know this city like I know the back of my hand. I thought she would like that we are on the same page, but the scowling look she is giving me suggests otherwise. "What?"

"If you knew that already, why the hell did you let me waste all this time?" She motions over the table in frustration.

"You were double checking my work. I would have been more worried if you got a different answer."

"Let's get one thing straight, detective Wolfe. We're supposed to be working *together* on this case. Even though I don't need you and can solve it on my own. So next time, maybe you could save the smug look and just tell me the information."

"Okay, Miss Smarty-pants. If I had told you we were going to Sears, you would have jumped my shit. Telling me that is just some assumption I made, and I was wrong. Then we would have still been here with that map, waiting for you to get to the same damn answer. So, I tried to cut out one argument. Just to find myself in another one." I clank my fork down on the plate.

"Right. Cause you know everything. Just like you always do." She crosses her arms and sits back, glaring at me. "You're Joe Wolfe." She starts in by saying my name in a mocking tone. "Perfect at everything. Knows what's best and thinks being some Podunk detective makes him better than the FBI."

"Uh, huh. Says little miss alphabet soup rookie that got dumped into Podunk nowhere. You're the one in my backyard, honey."

"I'm not your honey, and if you think I don't know this town, you're sorely mistaken. You don't even know my name, *stud*."

"Hrmph," I give her a taste of her own medicine. But that nagging feeling that I have had this very argument with her before strengthens. Who the fuck is this girl?

"Hmph!" She gives it back in spades. How do women do that? I don't really want to know. I just shake my head and throw the twenty on the table for breakfast.

"C'mon, Alphabet Soup. We got a parkin' lot calling our names." I wait long enough for her to gather up all the paperwork and map before following her out of the diner. I stop at the counter to pick up the two capped cups of Joe that Connie left us. This is going to be a long day.

Sears is on the other side of town. I spend the time tuning the radio to the local Christmas station as we make our way to the department store. The AM station runs classic Christmas music non-stop from December first to Christmas. "Sleigh bells ring, are you listenin'," pipes through the speakers in Bing Crosby's crooning voice. She rolls her eyes and looks out the window.

"What? You don't like Christmas music? I thought everybody loved Christmas."

"Christmas has nothing to do with that audio torture."

"Audio torture? This is classic Bing. I mean this is Bing at his prime." That gets her to pull her sulking gaze from the window and gawk at me.

"Are you seriously going to make me listen to this crap all day?" I can see the hint of fear on her face.

"Okay. This is not crap. It takes real vocal talent to do. Have you ever tried singing this song? Kicks my ass every time."

"I have and no, it doesn't take talent to belt out this garbage of fake cheer."

"Wow. Okay, Mister Scrooge. We have a bah-hum-bugger in the house."

"That's Miss Scrooge to you," Trouble barks back at me.

"Suit yourself. Just remember, Scrooge even loves Christmas in the end." I wink at her as I reach over to turn up the radio.

# CHAPTER THREE
## *You Better Watch Out*

I have to admit, torturing her with Christmas music all day has been the highlight of my week. She is a trooper, though. Not once did she reach over to change the station. We sat in this car and watched the poor schmuck ringing his heart out at the entrance. I was feeling pretty smug this morning about being right on the next location and having her confirm it. It meant we both knew how to do our job. The longer we sat here though, the less confident I felt. When the sun started to set, I huffed and shifted my weight for the hundredth time.

"Relax, Wolfe. All the attacks happened after sundown, anyway. We're just looking to see if anyone is watching Santa here other than us."

"Well, that's obvious. So, FBI? What made you want to become a fed?"

"I thought it would take me far, far away from Kansas City."

"What do you have against this town?" The sudden pride in my home town welling up. There is nothing wrong with the big KC.

"The people in it."

"Okay. You're going to have to be more specific. What kind of people? We talkin' people people? Purple people? Green people?" I give her the most serious of looks, "Purple people eaters?"

"You're an ass," she says as she lets a laugh escape before locking it back under the stern Agent Harris gaze.

"I am being serious. Is it purple and eats people? Or does it eat purple people?" I continue to have a very stoic expression on my face. I watch her bite her lip to stifle the laughter. Her face turns red, and her shoulders shake from the internal giggling I can see. Then she lets out the laugh.

"The parent people kind."

"Ah, the great birthers! Overbearing, over-doting, underachieving?"

"You have no idea who I am, do you?" She looks amused.

"No ducking the question. What kind of parents?" I give her a side-look. She is right. I have no clue who she is, and it's eating me up.

"Disapproving and disappointed. I did not become a teacher, a nurse, a rich man's wife, or a lawyer. In that order, specifically."

"Really? Well then, you got off easy."

"Right," her tone drips with sarcasm. "Because the Great Joe Wolfe had so much pressure to perform."

"I mean, literally, the bar was set at 'don't be a draft dodger'. Kind of hard to screw that one up." I shrug. I had my older brother, Billy, to thank for that.

"I figured you would've followed in your old man's footsteps."

"What? And become a history teacher? Meh. I didn't like school when I was in it. Why would I want to go back on purpose?" This gets a laugh from her again.

"I meant the army, jackass."

"Hrmph. Okay, I'll throw it back on your plate. Why didn't you follow in mommy dearest's footsteps?"

"Hmph."

"You know that's not actually an answer, right?" There is a long silence between us as she ignores my question. We both resume watching the guy ringing the bell. I can't take the silence. I break first.

"Can't even imagine how annoying that would be. Listening to the bell ring for eight hours. I can't even stand it just walking into the damn store." I tap my hand to the beat of the music on the steering wheel.

"But you'll listen to that shit?" She motions to the radio.

"When it comes with figgy pudding, hell yah. Wait. Have you ever had figgy pudding? What is figgy pudding? Now I want some."

"Seriously, Wolfe? Don't you have a chef in that baseball team sized family of yours?"

"I mean, Tristan enjoys dabbling. Don't know if he has ever made it to figgy pudding. I'll have to ask him to do that this year." The fact she knows so much about my family doesn't put me off. My father is pretty well known in these parts. I mean, war hero, state and federal representative, and beloved high school teacher. That man can do no wrong in the eyes of some of these people.

"You do that. Look, he's packing it up for the night." She motions to where the bell ringing has stopped.

We wait until the man has actually left and drive back to the station. It's a little past ten o'clock when I turn the keys in. We head back in to the bullpen and she returns the case files to my desk, newly marked map included. I lock everything up. She stops at the front desk, and I hear her ask for the phone. She dials a number and then waits patiently.

A moment later, she says, "Hello. Yes. I would like to have a cab pick me up." I cross my arms and tilt my head. Why would she be ordering a cab? Didn't she have her own car? "What do you mean it will be an hour? There aren't that many people in this city." She gives a sharp breath and then grumbles. "Fine, one hour. I'm not paying for your drive over here either."

I grin as I saunter over and pluck the receiver from her hand. "Cancel the car. She won't be needing it." I then hand the phone to the man behind the desk, and he hangs it up.

"What the fuck, Wolfe?"

"I'm giving you a lift." I smile. "But if you don't want it," I motion to the phone. "Good luck gettin' that cab before midnight on this side of town." I watch as her expression goes from shocked to angry to murderous in no time flat. I am pretty sure if we weren't in a police precinct she would punch me. She might still.

"Okay. Fine. But no funny business. These assholes already think I'm fuckin' the bureau chief."

"Yah. We both know that ain't true. If you were, you wouldn't be on this shit case." I flash her a grin and turn to head to my car. I can hear the guys behind the desk chuckling. Then there it is, the mystical girl grunt again. I am learning that inflection means something different when she uses it. I try not grin like an idiot when she trots up next to me to keep pace. A few minutes later, we're pulling out of the parking lot, and I turn the car to The Wolfe's Den.

"My apartment is that way," she points in the other

direction from where I turned.

"I'll get you there, eventually. First, a detour."

"Wolfe," she growls at me.

"What? You'll like it."

"Hmph."

"You know. Keep that up, and it'll freeze in place one of these days."

"HMPH," and she crosses her arms like a petulant child. It's not long before we are pulling into the parking lot of my uncle's bar. It is obvious it is a cop bar by the line of blue and white vehicles parked outside.

"After the shit show we sat through today, I don't know about you, but I need a drink. You can stay out here if you want. It's gonna get cold, fast." I kill the engine and ease out.

"A bar. Really? I am not drinking with you," she informs me as she gets out of the car.

I grin at her and head into the bar, taking up my usual spot at a table. I knew when Trouble walked into the bar as all the boys erupted into wolf whistles and catcalls. Most of those boys knew better, seeing as they are married, or old enough to be her father. I raise my hand up to signal for two beers when she plops down across from me with a sulk.

"Assholes, all of them. Can't they see I'm an agent?"

"Doesn't matter to them. All they see is a fine piece of work come walking through that door." She gives me an eyeroll and shakes her head. The beers are set before us and then Hatchett and Cleaver come walking up.

"Look at what we have here. Didn't even take you a day, Wolfe." Hatchett teases.

"To what? Share a drink with my partner? I hear it took you boys all of an hour before you were down here. At least we're off the clock." I smirk up at the asshole before me.

"Right. *Partners*," Cleaver chimes in. "Didn't realize escorts were a thing in the FBI now."

I sip my beer and chuckle as she comes up out the chair ready to box. This is going to be interesting.

"Listen here, cow paddy. Call me a whore again and I'll put you in the wall. Got it?" She gets right up in his face, brandishing a finger at him. I see her shift her beer in her other hand to make it a weapon.

Cleaver laughs right in her face and Hatchett joins in. He then turns to me and smirks. "This one's a spitfire. Got your work cut out for ya, Wolfe."

"Yah. That spitfire's about to bust you upside the head, you keep on like this." I nod to Trouble, whose eyes have narrowed to a dangerous slit as she contemplates wasting perfectly good beer on this idiot.

"Sit your asses down and leave the lady alone. You're not gettin' anywhere with her, and you know it." Thankfully, my uncle knows how to diffuse the situation. The room erupts into chuckling, and we all settle back down. Some poor kid with a guitar thinks he can play and gets up on the makeshift stage in the corner. It's not even a stage, really. It's a stool, next to a microphone with a gap between tables for the performer. I lean forward, watching Trouble.

"Ignore them idiots. Most of them wouldn't know how to talk to a girl if she climbed up into their lap and sat down."

"I doubt that kind of girl would talk," she takes a large swig of her beer.

"True. Bad analogy. My bad. So. Back to my question. Why didn't you follow in mommy's footsteps?"

"Tell you what, Wolfe. You out drink me tonight and I'll tell you whatever you want to know. But if I win. You shut the fuck up about my family, and I pick the music tomorrow."

"Oh, hell no! We're not not listening to Christmas songs." With a smirk I catch the bartender's eye and motion. He gives a nod and a minute later the flights of shot glasses are set before each of us.

"Here are the rules," she says. "Have to drink them all. No puking. No sloshing. If we tie, we order another flight. Got it?"

"If that's the way you want to roll," I say as I slam back the first shot. It's the cheap whiskey. The kind that just burns and has no real taste. It will definitely get you drunk, but you're going to regret in the morning. I thought for sure I'd have her on the whiskey.

Like I said, she's Trouble.

She throws that whiskey shot back like it is sweet tea and even makes a point of turning the glass upside down on the table with a clank.

"You hate Christmas music that much?" I eye her as I pick up the next shot and throw it back with gusto.

"I do right now." She grins and matches me.

"So, you admit you like Christmas music?" I snatch up the third shot.

"I plead the fifth," as she is already setting her third glass down.

"Oh, we both know that means you're guilty. Innocent people never plead the fifth." Four shots down. We're drawing a crowd at this point. I see money hitting the table and another flight is being set in front of each of us. She downs the fourth shot and smirks, reaching for number five. "What? No witty comeback? Plus, Christmas music is as American as apple pie." I slam back the last shot of the first flight.

19

"It's adorable you think you're witty." She slams her final shot of the first flight and the men around are now chuckling at us.

"'C'mon, Wolfe. Put this fed in her place! Awoo!"

"Awoo," she practically purrs at me as she reaches for shot number six. It's probably the hottest thing I have ever heard.

"You're still gonna have to listen to Christmas music. My car, my driving, my music," as I slam back shot six.

"Not your car. I'm driving, and you're gonna suck it up, buttercup." She snags shot seven. Jesus, this girl can drink. I feel like I am being played, but I'm digging it. She has relaxed and hell, it's kind of fun to see where this goes.

"Do you like, hate Christmas or something?" I slur as seven goes down the hatch.

"Hmph. I have to pee," she starts to get up.

"Ah! You leave the table you lose!" I shout it far too loud. "That means Christmas music until Christmas!" I laugh as she sits back down.

"That's not what we agreed on," she giggles. She takes shot eight and eyes it before drinking it.

I pick up number eight for me and hold up dramatically. "So what? I changed it! It's Chrismas," I slur, "Means chrimasusic," and number eight goes down the hatch. I am breathing a little harder and I have singed all of my taste buds off with the amount of whiskey we have shot in the past ten minutes. I cannot look away from her. Her cheeks are flushed, and in spite of her scornful retorts, she is grinning. I see her squirm, then give a girlish giggle. Her fingers curl around shot nine, and then shot ten.

Jesus, she's going to get us killed. I don't think I can do another round and she is determined to not listen to Christmas music. I have completely forgotten the rest of the bet. I watch in fascination as she slowly gulps down nine, takes a breath, then throws back ten triumphantly. Two can play at this game. I do not hesitate as I throw back nine and ten.

"Yous surindur," comes out, but I was trying to ask if she surrendered.

"Never!" she squeaks. "You are not going to beat me, Elijah!" She erupts into giggling as she says my first name. I know the sound of that giggle.

"Noelle?" I squint at her as if she were far away.

"Elle," she barks at me and gives me the dirtiest of looks.

"Joe," I bark back trying to match her look.

"Deal! Now, I'm gonna go pee." Then she races off to the bathroom.

"AWOO!" I call to the room. "Kissmas Music!" Then I stagger up to go use the restroom myself.

## CHAPTER FOUR
### *Come All Ye Faithful*

I knew it was a bad idea to follow her. I can hear the whooping and hollering behind me as I pass into the dimly lit hallway. I've never been the sharpest tool in the shed, especially when it comes to women. I could still pick up the faint scent of her perfume, but that could have been due to being trapped in a car with her all day. I dig the scent. I finish my business at the urinal in the men's bathroom and get cleaned up. The hallway is narrow, and I'm a decently sized guy. I nearly collide with her.

Then she giggles.

I am done for. I look down at those perfect pouty lips and her scent surrounds me. All I can think about is how much I would like to taste the alcohol that might still be on her lips. I lean in, keeping her trapped against the door.

"Wolfe," falls from her lips like a prayer. I am instantly hard. She can call me whatever she likes if she keeps talking like that. My hand slides from the door and down to her hip, pulling her closer. I say nothing as I smirk at her. We are both too drunk to make good choices and I'm going to regret this in the morning, I'm sure. For now, I am claiming my prize for saving Christmas tonight.

"Harris," I say with the hint of a question about what I intended to do to her. I wait only a moment before I tilt my head down and brush my lips against hers. I draw her into the kiss slow and sweet. I'm not a dick all the time. She punches my dance card then. Her fingers curled around the tie I had forgotten all about and pulls me into a more frantic kiss. The bathroom door opens from our weight and she's pulling me into the bathroom with her. Whatever thoughts I had about how she was probably a prude are thrown right out the window as I feel her press against me, rubbing that sweet little body against mine while she devours me with a needy kiss.

I don't say a word. There is no talking in bar sex. I am too drunk to hold her up properly while facing her. Not while she's wearing pants. I break our battle for tongue domination, and I smirk at her. With all the expertise of my time on the streets as a beat cop, I whirl her around and shove her against the full-length mirror near the door. When had my uncle put that in here? My one hand plants firmly between her shoulder blades to keep her held in place while the other hand flicks over the deadbolt on the door. I do not want to be interrupted.

Trouble lets out a little whine of a noise and grinds that perfect ass against me, causing me to grin. She's not trying to stop. She's egging me on. I lean in and roughly nip against her neck. I hungrily slide my hands along her waist until I'm unfastening the slacks and diving my fingers underneath to find cotton panties. It drives me insane to think she's this dirty but wearing the cutest cotton panties. I'll have to check later to see if they're some girly color, like pink. I bet they're pink and look sexy as hell on her. My fingers pop the band enough for my hand to slide underneath the fabric while my other hand gives a rough tug, sending her pants to her ankles.

"Hands up." I growl as I nip her earlobe. When she does not respond, I stroke her clit harder, intentionally being rough.

"Now."

I smirk as she brings her hands up on either side of the mirror. Fuck, this girl is hot as hell. Could she really be little Noelle Harris? I don't linger on it much as I take my free hand and hastily work my belt and pants, allowing them to drop to my knees as I pull myself free of my boxers. My other hand never stops working her. The fingers sliding and rubbing in a steady motion until I get her hips rolling nicely. Then I dare to dip my fingers into her, imagining my cock already buried deep. Maybe it's the whiskey, but right now I don't think I could ever get enough of this.

I finally tug her panties down in a forceful gesture, leaving that perfect little ass open to me. She is gasping as I kick her feet further apart and then, with little thought to her state I grab hold of my already aching dick and rub it along her until I feel the sweet spot where she draws me in. I thrust hard until I'm buried as far as I can go. She moans like a pornstar. Then she tilts her head back and I buck my hips against her as I bring up my other hand to lightly encircle her throat. I take my gaze from her reluctantly to look in the mirror. I expected to see her eyes closed and she be shy.

I should have known better. Trouble's eyes are staring right back at me in that mirror. It's a challenge as she grinds back against me. I smirk. As much as she has given me shit today, she wants this. She wants me to fuck her hard in this cramped bathroom with the blues music blaring from the kid on stage. I lean back and pump into her without mercy. The slapping noise from me drilling her echoing off the bathroom wall. I couldn't stop now if I wanted to. The fact she was watching us in the mirror makes my dick twitch in excitement. She's a dirty girl. Her muscles tighten and her hands curl into fists as I do not let up. My hands come to her waist again and hold on for dear life as I keep pumping. Her muscles tighten and I smirk. She's going to go first. That's when I knew she was in it as bad as I am. I'll give her what she wants. I thrust in deep and hold her against me, grinding my hips against her as I feel her shudder.

"Joe," she cries out, and it sounds like angels singing.

I lose it completely, and with a final thrust I explode in her. We are both panting, and I feel her shudder again before I pull out of her roughly. I pull my boxers and pants up first, getting situated while I am still pinning her to the mirror. I lean down further, and I bite her ass playfully as I slide her panties back up her perfectly toned thighs, followed by her pants. I even lean against her as I fasten them for her. She still has not moved her hands from the sides of the mirror and I smirk.

"Such a good little agent," I then step away from her and unlock the bathroom door. The glance over my shoulder reveals her blushing as she leans against the mirror. I leave her in the bathroom to catch her breath, and I strut out like the big dog I know I am. That's probably the hottest thing I have done in a few years. No one is paying me much mind, and I scoop up my jacket as I head out to the car to wait.

Sure enough, a few minutes later, here comes Trouble. We still don't say a word to each other as she slides into the passenger seat of my Firebird. I'm imagining bending her over the hood of my car and I feel myself starting to get hard again. We shouldn't be driving, but I manage it. Her place is close to here, according to her. I'm not thinking about tomorrow morning. Or how either of us intends to explain her car still being at the bureau. It didn't matter.

I pulled into the spot she mentioned and we're out of the car pretty fast. I didn't ask if she wanted me to come up. She didn't stop me. I pin her to the door with a frantic kiss and it makes her giggle then push me off to get the door unlocked. Like a parched man, I drink her kisses as soon as we are in the apartment. My jacket hits the floor, followed by the shoulder holster. Her shoes and jacket join the pile. We stumble along, parading our path to her bedroom with our clothes until she's naked in front of me at the foot of her bed. I'm raging hard again and all I can think about is how much I want her legs wrapped around me.

I step forward and scoop her right up into my arms, forcing her legs to part as we fall onto the bed. My hands palm her ass and pull her up to meet me. She arches off the bed when I thrust deep into her. She fits like a fucking glove. My mouth devours a nipple and I pinch the other. She has the perfect round breasts. Her skin is flawless. I was going to ride her hard and go home. That was my intent.

Then she rolled us over. She leaned up, putting her hands roughly on my chest, leaning over me. Her hair still in the ponytail, but the dark ringlet fell over her shoulder. She smirks at me, and I grin back. There is no love in our fucking. She is riding me hard. Hard enough I have to hold her hips again and just enjoy the ride. Letting her work me inside her how she wants. I never thought I'd like the assertive type. I'm usually the one in control, but the more she claimed me, the more I willingly submitted. She leans up fully, and her hands roam freely over her chest, offering her breasts to me and then pinching her own nipples. My eyes widen then I lost it. I wasn't able to hold back. This hot little minx thrust down and milked me for all she had until I erupted inside of her again.

She slowed her motion, and I watch in complete awe. I was still hard enough, and she wasn't done. My hands gently glide along her thighs as she rolls her hips gently. It is insanely intimate and takes my breath away with how her expression gets lost in the moment's ecstasy. She gasps and then I felt her body shudder again. Then, as if all the energy had been sapped from her, she lies down on top of me. Her head resting against my shoulder without pulling herself off of me. It wasn't long before I was out of her, but by then she was sound asleep against me. I felt like I could take on the entire defensive line of the Kansas City Chiefs and she was out like a light. I'm grinning like a damn idiot when I finally succumb to sleep.

I am roused from sleep by the angry blare of an alarm clock. I groan. My head is pounding, and my mouth is dry. I blink a few times and panic rushes in when I don't recognize where I am. I sit up and look around. This place is still half in boxes, nothing showing who it belonged to. I frown as I remember exactly what happened. I look down at my naked self. I'm dirty as hell and every muscle is sore.

There are faint scratch marks on my chest. It makes me smirk. I shake my head and try to figure out where she went. Slowly, the hiss of the shower can be heard coming from behind the bathroom door. I swing my legs over the side of the bed and then I see it. The picture of little Noelle Harris with her brother, Skip, at Cocoa Beach the Spring break of my senior year of high school. I rub my hand over my face and stand fully.

By the time I hear the shower turning off, I am dressed and making sure there is nothing of mine left in this place. Sure, it was a dick move, but the last thing I needed was the captain throwing me off this case for breaking the rules. I turn the doorknob lock as I pull the door closed behind me and retreat to my car without looking back. I'd hit up my apartment, shower, change, and head to the station before anyone could even possibly think we spent the night together. Fuck, what was I thinking?

## CHAPTER FIVE
### *Do You See What I See*

I sit at my desk, trying not to feel guilty. Not about the sex, but about bailing on her when she didn't have a car. I should have at least given her a lift. If I left cash, she might deck me for treating her like a whore. I glance at the entrance for the hundredth time in as many minutes. No one seems to have put together what we did and where we went after the bar. Though Cleaver keeps giving me the stink eye. I wonder who pissed in his Wheaties to warrant that look. I turn to the map in front of me, giving it a once over. Sears is the only logical place for them to hit next based on the locations of the previous attacks. I glance at my watch and still no Trouble. I pick up the phone on my desk and ease her business card from under the paper-clip holding the file together. I don't have her home number, so office it is.

No answer.

I put the phone back in its cradle and tap my pencil in irritation. Was she at the bureau telling her boss what we did? I glance at the captain's office and see he is sitting at his desk in a calm state. That rules out she is tattling on us.

"Hey, fellas!" I hear her voice ring out behind me. It catches most of the bullpen's attention. "Brought breakfast," she chirps. I watch her like a hawk as she saunters around the room and holds the box out for each of these assholes to pick their favorite treat. She doesn't even look at me. One by one, each of the guys picks out a pastry. She reaches my little desk in the corner and picks up the apple fritter, my favorite, before depositing the empty box in the trash. I cock an eyebrow as she makes a show of taking a seat in the perp chair and savoring each bite of that fritter in front of me.

"Enjoying yourself, are you?" I say with a chuckle.

"Mhm hmm," as she has a mouthful. "Sorry, ran out," she mutters between bites. She's not sorry at all from the look on her face.

"Welp, now that you're here. It's time to go be bored to death watching a man ring a bell."

I definitely deserve the lack of sweet treat, but I wasn't going to let her know that. I snatch the keys I got from Gary behind the desk and ease up to leave. I'm riveted to the spot, as are a few other guys who notice her pop her finger in her mouth and suck it clean after eating the fritter. I shake my head and move on. She is so much Trouble.

"Hey, wait up!" She calls as she hurries to catch up. I notice she is using a napkin to clean the rest of her hand off when I didn't take the bait. I am not sure what's going on here. She does not seem to be too upset by what has happened. Was this a thing for her? Does that bother me? It's kind of hot now that I think about it. Fuck, now I'm thinking about it.

This is going to be a long day.

We rolled into Sears' parking lot thirty minutes later. You bet your bottom dollar I played Christmas music the whole way. She rolled her eyes at my choice of music but left it on the Christmas station. Good to know, she will uphold a bet. I feel smug in knowing she has accepted my win. The atmosphere in the car is lighter today. I even catch her grinning at my terrible rendition of the Chipmunk Christmas song. I love music, all kinds of music. But as my sisters keep telling me, I couldn't carry a tune in a five-gallon bucket with a lid. Doesn't matter, I still sing anyway. Then, as if summoned by me thinking about them, the sweet voices of Tabby, Rachel, and Nor, begin harmonizing Carol of the Bells. That's right, my super famous sex-kitten rockstar of a sister and the two goody two-shoes she conned into it, put out a Wolfe Sisters Christmas album. It's all the rage with the locals.

"Hey, isn't that your sister?"

"Sisters, plural," I correct.

She lets it go but looks amused. At hour four, I'm dying to know my performance score. I mean, I positive she liked it. She called my name and went for round two. Great, now I am thinking about her riding me and we're in this car for at least another three hours. I give her a side glance and she is smiling as she watches the bell ringer. I try to act casual as I keep steal side glances at her. It's hard to reconcile the chunky tomboy she was with the smoking hot agent sitting in this car.

A few hours later I am getting eager for conversation. She has said maybe five words all day. Was this the silent treatment? What do I care? This isn't my first one-night stand. Okay, I care. Normally, I don't have to work with them after the one night. "So... how's Skip?" I pick a neutral topic. Or at least what I thought was neutral.

"Skip's Skip. Still an asshole. What do you want to know about him? His current girlfriend's not your type. She's faithful."

Damn, Trouble's got a smart mouth. Was she always this snappy? Had I missed out back in high school on all that witty banter we could have had?

"He's a first year at Brigham, Swanson, and Terry. Her name is Mandy, and she has been Mr. Swanson's assistant for at least two years." I have to laugh at her mocking bubble gum sweet voice when referring to Mandy. "Mom and Pop adore her. She is about as smart as Cleaver." Then she falls quiet again, still watching the bell ringer. She doesn't ask me anything about my family, which makes me pout. Why am I pouting? What do I care if she doesn't ask? She's the rude one.

Then the bell ringer is packing up, and it's dark. I am sulking in the driver's seat. Not even the cheery Christmas music is helping. "I'm assuming you do not want to grab a beer tonight?"

"Awe, Wolfe, now you care about what I want to do? That's sweet. I mean, this morning, I got the message, don't call me, I'll call you."

"I panicked, okay!" I practically shout at her. Then she gets this smug little look on her face, like she has been waiting all day for me to broach this topic. Damn it. The silent treatment works!

"Don't get your panties in a knot, Wolfe. We're good. I called a cab to go get my car. And your captain might have a heart attack if he found out we fucked."

"I didn't think about that," I whispered to myself.

"I mean. The man is a walking heart attack. I don't think he knows what a vegetable is." She muses like we weren't just talking about fucking last night.

"Er... So... About that beer?" Why do I feel awkward? What

are they teaching them at the FBI? I feel like I did in high school when I wanted a girl's attention. I'm twenty-seven years old, damn it!

"Not tonight, Champ. I have plans. Let's get back to the station."

Did she just reject me? Who does she have plans with? I nod and drive us back to the station. She hops out of my car and gives me a little finger wave as she trots over to hers. I watch her the entire time trying to figure out what game she is playing and how I could win it. Or at least get an instruction manual. I've never met a woman like this. She doesn't even look back as she gets into the driver's seat.

A moment later, she is pulling out of the parking lot. I turn in the car for the night and think about heading over to the bar. I opt not to, as my head is still mildly throbbing from our misadventures last night. Boy, was I glad I decided not to drink myself stupid two nights in a row.

As I walked into the office the next morning, Elle was waiting at my desk, holding a small brown paper bag between two fingers. She shook it and grinned at me as if she were saying sorry for yesterday. How long had she been here? I figure out not long as the captain comes barging out of his office.

"Good, you're both here. Get your asses in here!"

She makes an eek face, but is grinning as well. I snatch the paper bag before she can change her mind and shrug. It's like we got caught playing hooky together and are being summoned to the principal's office. "Mornin', Cap'n," I say as I pop the apple fritter into my mouth. Trouble closes the door and takes a seat next to me. She sets a cup of coffee on the desk in front of me while she sips her own. She doesn't look too perplexed by his red-faced shouting.

"Whatever you two have been doing is bullshit. There's been another attack." He flops the folder in front of us.

We shoot each other a look, and both straighten up. She opens the file and frowns. "That's not the guy that was outside of Sears."

"Listen, sweet cheeks, when I want your opinion, I'll ask for it. Otherwise, sit there and look pretty. Let the big boys handle it."

"Hmph." She then turns to me, ignoring the captain, as she picks up the file. "I'll be at your desk. Doing real work while he wags his dick at you some more." With that, she stands and leaves the room, like nothing happened.

Damn, she's sexy as hell when she dishes it out. My pants get uncomfortable until I turn to look at the captain. His angry face solves that problem real quick.

"What the hell are you waiting for, Wolfe? An engraved invitation? Get your ass back to work."

I am up out of that chair like lightning. As I close the door, I hear a parting shout.

"No fucking!"

I can't help myself, and I smirk, as I think it's too late for that. When I get to my desk, she's not there, neither are the files. I look around the room to see she has commandeered the empty windowed office that has a corkboard on the wall we usually play darts at, and a dirty chalk board with a bum caster. Spread out on the table is the map she had marked up. The stacks of papers are off to the side.

Her back is to me as I sit in front of the map. I take a moment to enjoy the heady scent of the black permanent marker before I take the ruler and connect all the dots she had meticulously plotted. After the third ear-splitting squeal the marker makes, she whirls around to see my handy work.

"You've ruined that map." She is laughing.

I do not respond to her mocking laugh as I finish connecting all the dots. She leans in, close enough I can tell that there is a delicate lace pattern on her bra.

"You know, you're kind of cute when you are focusing. You stick the tip of your tongue out of the side of your mouth. It's adorable." My last line squeaks off the map onto the table. I look up to her face and see her smirking at me. She absolutely knows where my eyes had been.

"Away with ye harlot! I'm done anyway." I give her a wolfish grin to show I am teasing. But damn, if she doesn't smell good too. Or it's the fumes from the marker I am still holding.

"You want to tell me why you ruined this perfectly good map?" She motions and then turns back to her task of hanging photos up on the wall of our victims.

"This, my dear Agent Harris," I say as I tap on the ruined map, "is pure chaos. Meaning that we are back to square one." I huff as I lean back in the squeaky office chair and toss the marker onto the map.

"Mhm hmm," she says without turning around. She has all but one picture up when I noticed it.

"I'll be damned. Do you see what I see?"

# CHAPTER SIX

## *We Need a Little Christmas*

"Really, Wolfe? Still with the Christmas shit? And stop looking at my ass." She growls at me without looking back.

I smirk. As perfect as her ass is, and as hilarious as the pun was, I had asked in earnest. "No, Harris, look at the wall. What do all our victims have in common?" I could have just said it, but if she saw the pattern too, it would confirm what I think is going on. I watch her as she steps back and leans against the table. I lean back in my seat and give her a minute.

"They're all Santas."

"Yup. And our bell ringer at Sears, was not."

"So, how do they determine who is Santa?" She turns around and starts shuffling through the stacks of paper like a crazy person.

"What're you doin', Harris?" I stand up to come help her in her shuffling.

"Looking for the volunteer sheet. To ring the bell, they have to fill out an application and they are coordinated by a single contact. Oh, what's her name?" She keeps moving through the papers quickly. I pick up a stack and start thumbing through as well. Then she exclaims, "Mrs. Gayle! Here we go! Up for an adventure?"

"Always," I grin and the pair of us are out the door before the captain can say anything about leaving all our stuff in the war room. We get into the parking lot, and I head to my car. She heads to hers. As if we were thinking the same thing, we stop and stare at each other. I think of the Good, the Bad, and the Ugly, and smirk at her again. "Nuh uh. My lead, my car."

"Hell, no. My info, my car!" She comes back just as cocky and waggles the paper with the address on it at me.

"Fine. But we're still listening to Christmas music." I grin as I start toward her car.

"The hell we are. You touch my radio; I'll break your fingers."

"Hey! Are you telling me Noelle Harris is the kind of person to renege on a bet?" My smile stays innocent as I watch her eyes narrow at me. I definitely got under her skin with that comment.

"Elle. We agreed. Fine! But then you're buying lunch."

I hold up my hands in innocent surrender to the correction. "Deal." As we approach the cherry red 1986 Jaguar XJ6, I give a low whistle. "Nice wheels, Agent Harris." I am on the wrong team if she can afford this.

"Thanks! Pop gave it to me for graduating." She slides into the driver's seat and I get in the passenger's side. The inside held a hint of pipe tobacco, and her perfume. At this rate, I'm never getting her out of my head and now all I can think about is getting her into the back seat. The devilish grin on my face makes her cock an eyebrow at me.

"What?" She asks.

"Nothin'," I reply as I reach for the radio. She literally slaps my hand away before changing the station herself.

"I told you not to touch my radio."

We talk little on the way to meet with Mrs. Gayle. I watch out the passenger window, bopping along to Chuck Berry's song. I notice her fingers bopping on the steering wheel as well. I'll melt that Grinch's heart yet.

It didn't take long to get to the building where the bell ringers gather. People are coming and going with buckets and bells. More than one person takes a double take at her Jaguar, and she chuckles about it. They are working out of an old church's parish that has been converted to public space. The line circles around the room meticulously. I notice there is an unholy amount of Christmas cheer in this place. Little angels, stars, and at least three trees, coupled with a manger scene stuffed on every horizontal surface possible. All of them are different. How many ways can Jesus be born?

"Pay attention, Wolfe. Or you might get turned into a wiseman," Trouble jokes under her breath. I snort my laugh and the two of us saunter up to the table where an elderly woman is standing. Her ruddy brown hair has faded to a pepper of blond and silver. Her eyes are hidden behind large glasses, and her earrings are massive Christmas trees that make her earlobes droop. Without making my sweeping gaze obvious, I take in the hideous holiday cardigan over a blouse with a neck scarf tied into a massive red bow. This gives way to a pleated green skirt. But the cherry on top, were the candy cane stockings with matching elf shoes that curled at the toe. The little jingle bells dangling from the point ring with every shift of her weight. This woman is Christmas cheer incarnate. She is absolutely adorable looking.

Then she spoke.

"You two. Back of the line. No cutting for Christmas!" Her voice is sharp and indignant that we would misbehave in her den of joyful cheer.

"Even if I have a special hall pass?" I flash my badge to get her attention. Agent Harris does the same.

"How can I help you, officers?" Her tone immediately changes.

"We're curious about your Santas," Elle starts.

"San-ta," Mrs. Gayle corrects. "There is only one Santa, thank you." She pushes her glasses up her nose as she looks down at Elle.

"Whatever. Where is San-ta ringing tonight?"

I then cough a little to deescalate the Santa-off. "What my partner here is trying to say, is do you have the schedule of appearances for Santa?"

Mrs. Gayle lights up as it dawns on her why we are here. "Oh! Bless you! You're looking into why someone would be so naughty as to attack Santa, aren't you? Took you long enough! Right this way. I have been calling that other naughty policeman, and he just won't listen to me. I am glad someone is finally taking me seriously. Julie, please take over bell duty." She hands the bored looking teenage girl forced into her elf uniform her clipboard and pen before she turns and motions for us to follow her. Elle and I cannot help but grin at each other as she jingles down the hallway. The tiny bells magically are in time with the ever present Christmas music flooding from a boom box somewhere.

She leads us into her office. Mrs. Gayle is the woman who keeps *everything*. From children's hands painted in prayer to papier mâché Jesus, I am convinced we're in a firetrap. She scurries around the stacks of hymnals and Bibles to get to her side of the desk. I allow Elle to enter next, while holding the door. "Such a gentleman," Elle mutters at me. Our eyes meet and we cannot keep the grins off our faces.

"Now. I trust that the two of you will guard Santa's secret well. He is a very busy man, and his schedule cannot be interrupted." She is holding a piece of paper in her hand as she looks up at us. Elle snorts but quickly recovers when Mrs. Gayle cuts her the dirtiest of looks. Santa is serious business to this woman.

"You have my word, Ma'am," I turn on the boyish charm that always gets the grandmas on my side.

"Good! Now, I have been incredibly careful with this. These boys are good boys! Helping Santa out like this. It is such a tragedy that they have been hurt." She hands me the paper and Elle is biting her lip to not say whatever she is thinking. "I expect you to solve this, young man. You must save Christmas."

"I will do my best, ma'am. I won't let you, or Santa, down." I give her my solemn vow. Elle is turning red with repressed laughter. We both give Mrs. Gayle a nod and turn to head out. Only, Mrs. Gayle was not done spreading Christmas cheer with us. She leads us back to the main area they are using for the buckets.

"Wait here," Mrs. Gayle commands as we start to follow her through an archway. I glance at Elle, and she shrugs, still biting her lip to keep her laughter locked inside. I watch the jolly display of Mrs. Gayle putter around the tiny area she is in and come back with two gift-wrapped treat bags with large paper tickets sticking out of them. "Since you're both on Santa's Nice List, here are your goodies! I hope you enjoy the show! Our kids have worked so hard for it." I notice that twinkle in her eye as she looks between us, then up. "Uh oh! Mistletoe!" Then she deftly ducks between us to leave us there.

I blink as I process the sudden onslaught of gifts, command, and setup. How did I walk right into this trap? My eyes find Elle's and she has the same dumbfounded look I have. Our cheeks flush hot and we can hear the hen circle giggling in the other room.

"Awe, what's the matter, Wolfe? Afraid of a little mistletoe?" Trouble's voice purrs at me. We're in a church, for God's sake. But now she has thrown down the proverbial gauntlet. In a swift and easy motion, I wrap my arm around her and draw her up on her toes as if I am going to have my way with her in this doorway. I lean in close, gazing longingly into her eyes, and I place a sweet, chaste peck on her lips before letting her go and turning to walk away.

"Asshole," I hear her whisper behind me. I cannot help the smug look that spreads across my face.

Once outside of the church, Elle bowls over, laughing. "Oh man, Santa. So serious," she gasps between guffaws. "And what was that? You call that a kiss?" She teases.

"In front of those hens? You wanted me to bend you over the counter in front of them? We both know where real kisses go." I wriggle my brows at her. Then the sweetest thing happens. Elle Harris blushes bright red and goes quiet. After the awkward moment between us in silence. "Well. Okay then," I mumble as I now blush.

"Shut up, Wolfe," she punches my arm. "Where are we heading?"

I cough and follow her to the car. "Children's Palace. Toy store near the mall. Kansas side."

An hour later, we are parked where we can see Santa ringing his sleigh bells with great gusto. There is an odd tension in the car, which amuses me. I can't explain it, but I get the odd sense there is something more going on here. With the scowl at the corner of her eyes, there is no way in hell I am broaching that topic. I hum along happily with the carols on the radio.

After about three hours, she jerks open the door and gets out. "I'll be back," she mutters as she slams the door. I watch her practically stomp to the hot chocolate stand set up just for the holidays. She kind of walks like Daffy Duck when she is mad. I really shouldn't be laughing. It's just so damn adorable. She sure is pissed, which is hilarious. I turn my attention back to Santa and relax.

I finally find a comfortable position when all hell breaks loose.

# CHAPTER SEVEN
## *Run Rudolph Run!*

When I say all Hell breaking loose what I mean is I see agent Harris toss her cups of hot chocolate and take off running like a madwoman. It does not take me long to see why she is running. Fifteen feet in front of her is a scrawny kid with a red bucket hauling ass around the corner. A quick glance back at Santa, and the shoppers near him tell me all I need to know. I hop over the console and slide into the driver's seat. I can't help but take a moment to enjoy the feel of the steering wheel. "This is going to be fun," I smirk as I throw it into gear.

I only squeal the tires a little as I race to catch up to the hot foot chase. I'm hindered by the angry housewives glaring at me as I fly through the parking lot. It's not long though before I can round that corner and push the pedal to the metal. The Jaguar purrs sweeter than Elle did the other night.

"Damn, that kid's fast."

It does not help he is cutting through back alleys to lose Agent Harris. She's damn fast, too. I try to keep up as best I can, but I'm not about to damage this beauty.

The whole thing took about five minutes before I see Elle

picking herself up from the pavement, along with a little red bucket, with no perp in sight. The look she is giving me would murder a lesser man. I ease the Jaguar into park and hop out.

"You alright?"

"Good news is, we got the bucket."

"So, what's the bad news?"

"Kid's got springs and jumped the fence. I lost him in the alley."

"Well, damn," I mutter as I take the bucket from her. We file back into the car.

"It's okay, Jerome. I won't let him hurt you again," I hear Elle say as I am easing into the passenger seat. She is petting her dashboard.

"Do you name all your cars?"

"Of course. Don't you?"

"No, not really. Jerome?"

"Yes. Jerome. Don't drive my car." She pulls out into traffic.

"Well, if I hadn't been driving your car you would have had one hell of a walk back to Santa."

"Shit. We need to go talk to Santa." I grip the door as she pulls a hairpin U-turn right there in the middle of traffic. The way she drives, tells me she has bigger balls than any guy I have ever met.

By the time we get back to Santa, the EMTs have already checked him out and cleared him. There are a couple of my buddies from the beat hanging around.

"Get anything useful?" I ask as we come rolling up.

"Nah. Guy says he was ringin' the sleigh bells, then got knocked upside the head. You know anything about an FBI agent chasing the perp?"

I give a grin and slowly look from the beat cop to Agent Harris. "Would you like to take this one, Agent Harris?"

"Asshole," she whispers to me as she puts in park and gets out to talk with the guys. I follow her and listen to her recounting of tonight's adventures. It takes a few minutes, but then Jerry, the guy on the beat grins at me.

"...Then he threw the bucket at me as he leapt for the fence. It was bucket to the face, or dodge." She shrugs, like it was a regular Tuesday night.

Jerry whistles a low whistle. "Damn, girl." He is impressed with her heroics. I am irritated. Had she radioed we would have had backup, but I don't steal her thunder on the street. "So, you got this report, Wolfe?" Jerry asks me with a big smile.

"Yah. Yah. I'll finish it up at the house."

"Of course you will. Don't you let him talk you into writing it up for him, either, Miss Harris."

"Agent. It's Agent Harris," Trouble corrects him.

"Yes, ma'am, Agent Harris."

We take his notes and get back in the car to take off. The Christmas music bops along on the radio, and I can see she is still pumping with adrenalin the way she taps the steering wheel as she drives.

"You know, we might have caught the guy had you radioed for backup." I throw the glove down for the whole 'we are a team' lecture.

"Are you fucking serious, Wolfe?"

"Only reason you had anyone to back you up is I saw you taking off like a bat out of hell. Otherwise, you would have been out there on your own."

"I can handle myself," she counters, and her tone is

defensive and angry.

"That is not the point. The point is you could have got shot. What if that asshole had a gun?" I shout at her.

"Really? The whole 'he could have shot you?' bullshit? Do you know, that statistically speaking, being shot in the line of duty is so rare? You know what? I don't answer to you, Wolfe. I did what I was supposed to do in the moment and the *only* reason you are giving me shit is I don't have a dick!" She shouts right back.

"Nuh uh. Nope. If you had called for backup like you were supposed to do, then we would have had an entire fleet going after that punk and got his ass. You can't tell me that when that bastard turned around and chucked that bucket at your head that you... you..." I sputter for a moment as I try to form a rational sentence in my rage fueled concern.

It takes a few seconds, but I start again with a more coherent thought, "You cannot tell me when he turned, that the idea of him pulling a gun on your ass didn't flash through your mind." I shake my finger at her in an accusing manner.

"When he turned, asshole, he had one hand on the fence, and red bucket weighing him down. I damn well knew, even if he had a gun, he wasn't shootin' anybody with it. And I don't fucking care if he had an oozy. I would still have chased him down. I almost had him. Had I stopped to radio you fucking doughnut eaters, he still would have fled. And *we* wouldn't have the bucket. Do you really think, some Santa punching punk isn't going to be in the system? So, get off your fucking high horse, *detective*, and maybe realize I don't fucking have a KCPD radio. You want me to pull a damn phone out of my ass?"

"What do you mean, you don't have a KCPD radio? We

issued you one when you walked in the damn door."

"The fuck you did."

"God damn it, Carl. I'm going to fucking kill him." I mutter as I cross my arms and sulk. I don't blame her for running after the perp. I would have done the same damn thing. I have no leg to stand on if she doesn't have a damn radio to begin with. How did I miss that? I frown as I realize just how dangerous that situation could have been. First thing in the morning, I am going to read Carl the riot act. I can tell she is fuming behind the wheel. All bravado has stopped between us and the only sound is the raucous merriment of Chuck Berry.

She rolls up alongside the curb in front of the station, puts her foot on the brake and does not even put it in park. Next thing I know, she is reaching across me to open up the passenger door and flinging it open.

"Get the bucket into evidence." Her tone is ice.

I do not argue with her as I hotfoot it out of the car with the bucket. She roars away just as the door closes.

"Well then," I lift the bucket and look at it, "what the hell am I going to do with you? I guess all you're good for is being thrown at the head of my partner... by the perp." My eyes light up as I realize what she was saying in the car. "I wonder if the nerds are still here." I turn and trot up the steps into the precinct house.

The next morning, I am sitting at my desk bright and early, and I even have an extra fritter just for her. At a quarter till eight, she comes storming in like a winter blizzard. Even the bullpen takes pause as she blows right by me and slams the war room's door closed. I pick up my gifts for her after letting out a heavy sigh. This was going to be rough. I can see her from my desk. She has plopped into a chair and is sitting ram-rod straight with her arms crossed. Her fingers drumming angrily on her forearm as she stares at the Santa wall. It takes me a moment to get into the war room, having to manage the awkward jumble of gifts I have brought for her this morning.

"I have presents for you," I chirp as I saunter up to her. I then place the bag containing the fritter, a cup of coffee, a cup of hot chocolate, the KCPD radio I had issued for her, and a manila file folder. I was not sure if she drank hot chocolate, but she had seemed excited about getting one last night. Without another word, I move to the other side of the table and take a seat to see her reaction.

There is something intrinsically beautiful about the stormy look in her eyes as she stares at me. She ignores the fritter, drink, and radio, to open the folder without a word. After she reads through the documents in front of her, "What the fuck, no useable prints? Did they test the fucking handle?" She growls at the evidence log copy in front of her.

"I know, right? Cost me two cases of good beer to get that thing rushed. For them to come up with bupkis..." I had watched as those guys poured over every surface possible on that bucket. "There was a whole bunch of partials. After they ruled out all of us, there was nothing left that was usable. There have been a lot of people who have touched that bucket." I huff as I cross my arms.

She huffs too and leans back. I smile when I see her reach for the fritter. "So now what?" She asks between bites.

## CHAPTER EIGHT
### *Here Comes Santa Claus*

"Wolfe! Harris! My office, now!" The captain roars and causes the flimsy window walls of the war room to rattle. I shake my head and know we are about to get our asses chewed again. Elle stuffs the fritter into her mouth and does her best chipmunk impression as she snags the coffee to chase it down. I hold the door open for her and then I watch her as she walks by me toward the other room. It's then I notice the faint circles under her eyes and the red tint to them. I knew that look. I have six sisters. Elle Harris has been crying. Now I feel even more like an asshole than I did after she told me she didn't have a radio.

I close the captain's door behind me and come to stand alongside Elle when we get into his office.

"I don't know what the fuck I was thinking. This was a mistake." I watch him pace behind his desk, his face growing as red as Santa's suit. He stops and looks between the two of us. "What did I tell you, Wolfe?"

He spits as he shouts, and we shift to avoid it. I open my mouth to speak, and the faint shake of Elle's head tells me to keep quiet. I raise a brow but hold my tongue. I can see her

49

jaw clenching, and her posture says she had expected this tear down. I know the captain well enough to know if he's screaming, he's harmless. He just likes to feel like he's in control.

"Are you two fucking? Is that why you were in an unsanctioned car without radios?" He snarls, and I imagine the entire bullpen is standing outside the door.

"Captain," I start to defend us.

"Shut the fuck up, Wolfe." He slams his fist down on the desk.

"No, sir," Elle's voice cuts across the room in a polite and firm tone. "We were in my car because I didn't follow procedure. It's my fault we lost the guy. Don't blame Wolfe. Kick me off the case if you want, but Wolfe's got an idea that my boss thinks will solve the case."

I watch the captain, keeping a straight face, and not giving away the feeling of my jaw hitting the floor from her bald-faced lie. She did not even give me a second glance. The captain's range of emotions went from rage to astonishment, then to curiosity. "Oh? Just what the fuck has this asshole come up with?"

Yes, just what the fuck did I come up with?

"He's going to be the next Santa. They're targeting the Santas. He poses as Santa, rings the bells, and when the kid attacks him, we grab him." She says it as if it were obvious that's the next step. She just pulled that out of her ass. But, to be fair, it is obviously the next step.

"That's assuming he'll strike again. What if your little stunt scared him off?" The captain points a pudgy digit at her like an angry sausage.

"If it goes to shit, blame me, and KCPD loses nothing." I

don't know how the fuck she does that. But the captain's face shifts from apoplectic red to his normal flush color. I am beginning to think she has some kind of superpower. "I mean, I'm just a skirt playing cop, right?" Then she took it there.

The captain's eyes narrow, and he picks up the phone. We stood in silence as he dialed and waited. I am trying to will her to look at me so we can have a silent conversation about what the hell was happening. She doesn't look at me. She holds her chin up in defiance, and I see the way she is biting her cheek to keep from smirking.

"... So, you agree then? You want to put this knucklehead in a Santa suit and see if the perp'll take the bait again? Fine. But if your agent fucks this up again, I'm throwing you all under the bus." He slams the phone down into its cradle. "You, missy." He grumbles. "I don't know how you did that. You must be good at something over there." His eyes trail from her face down.

My head whips up at what the captain just insinuated, and I tense. My hand curls into a fist with the sudden urge to defend her honor. Yah, she's a looker, and sure, she fucks like a porn star. But I'll be damned if she is not a great fucking agent. She did not even hesitate out there. I open my mouth to tell him off, but she speaks again.

"Yes, sir. We have permission to do it, then?" I can see the red tint in her cheeks from embarrassment, or fury, I can't tell because she has a stone cold poker face otherwise. I am never playing poker with this woman.

"You're on thin ice, Agent Harris. Fuck this up, and I'll make sure the only thing you're pushin' is paper. Get out." He flops into his chair.

I follow Elle back to the war room like a lost puppy. This

girl is under my skin. In the span of about five minutes, she went from pain in the ass fed to full on partner. She took all the blame and then gave me the credit for her fucking idea. "What was that about?"

"What was what about?" she asks with a coy smile.

"How the fuck you get your boss to agree to it?" I cross my arms.

"I didn't. He hates your captain."

"Wait. You're telling me, he straight up lied and agreed with whatever you said because the captain questioned it?"

"Yup," she smirks. I remind myself to never get on her bad side. She is brilliantly scary. "C'mon, let's get a car and get you fitted for your big debut, Santa Wolfe." She snatches up her radio and clips it on the waist of her pants.

I am flabbergasted by this turn of events and our ride to Mrs. Gayle's Santa headquarters is relatively quiet. I cannot help but grin when she tunes the radio to the Christmas music station.

Mrs. Gayle eyes the two of us suspiciously when we explain to her our plan. "I will have you know, being Santa is a *sacred* duty. Do you understand me, young man?"

"Yes, ma'am," I nod solemnly. Elle has returned to biting the inside of her cheeks to keep from laughing.

"I expect this suit to come back in pristine condition. No smoking. No eating. No drinking. No cologne after you have put it on. You will have it dry cleaned and returned to me no later than noon two days from now."

"Yes, ma'am."

"Wonderful! Now, let's get you fitted! Strip." Her musical voice chirps and I oblige.

Elle is smirking as she leans against the wall. I also hear the giggling of girls not too far off. The look on my face suggests I know exactly what they want to look at. I shrug and ease my jacket off, followed by the rest of my clothes until I am to my boxers. My thumb hooks into the waistband, and I hear the audible gasp from the hidden gaggle. I can't help but chuckle as Elle is looking at her fingernails, pretending to be disinterested, but I see her looking none the less.

"Young man! Put those back on! You're in a church, for Christ's sake!" I give her the boyish grin as I see her cheeks flush, too.

"Just following orders, ma'am. My apologies."

Elle snorts behind me.

"Yes, well. Hmm. Now that I have had a look at you, you're on the skinny side. So. Let me see."

I watch in horror as she does not move to the rack of red suits waiting. Instead, she plucks through a rack of morbidly flesh-colored bags with straps. It was like watching a butcher in a meat market.

"No. Too fat. Not enough. Hmm." She looks at me, then back at the flesh bags. "Ah ha! Put this on."

"And this is?" holding the bags at arm's length, feeling the heft in my hand.

"Santa's fat and Jolly, Wolfe. You look like Santa if he was starved for a year. What kid'll believe that?" Elle jabs. She is enjoying this way too much.

"Hmph," Mrs. Gayle interjects and motions for me to put it on.

I grumble and comply. The things I do for this job. A few minutes later I am dressed in the entire ensemble. My back is already starting to hurt. This outfit itches, and I am sweating up a storm in spite of it being frigid in this dressing room.

Then she hands me the Santa beard. I was expecting the beard, but not the hair. She insists to complete the outfit. So, I put them on. Thirty minutes of this torture goes by as I learn intimately there is a wrong way to put on fake hair and beards. Elle is snickering again. I am convinced she came up with this as revenge for yesterday. I am handed the sleigh bells, which are easily five pounds of wood and metal.

"Now. Let's hear your laugh, Santa." Mrs. Gayle demands.

"Ho. Ho. Ho." My delivery is a little flat and lackluster.

"Awe. C'mon, Santa Wolfe, you can do better than that. It's from the gut." Trouble chastises.

"I thought you didn't believe in Santa, *Noelle*." I grumble.

"I never said I didn't believe in Santa, *Elijah*. I said I hated Christmas carols. Do it right or get the fuck out and I'll call a fed to play Santa."

"Language, young lady," Mrs. Gayle snaps. "And you, Elijah, will ho, ho, ho properly, or not at all. When I say not at all, I mean no Santa suit."

I roll my eyes. Women. I dig deep, calling all my Christmas cheer to the surface, if only to escape this torture device they have dressed me in, and I bellow while holding my weird belly sack, "Ho! Ho! Ho! Merry Christmas!" It is a properly Jolly ol' Saint Nick belly laugh.

Mrs. Gayle lights up and claps. "Bravo! I knew you could do it, Elijah!"

"Yah. *Elijah*, fantastic job." Trouble's voice is dripping with sarcasm.

"Are you sure you don't want to be Mrs. Claus, Noelle, dear? I have the dresses and petticoats."

"I apologize, Mrs. Gayle. I have to make sure nothing

happens to Santa since he will not be in proper police attire. But thank you," Trouble gives me a grin as she weasels out of it.

"You two would make such a lovely Mister and Misses Clause. If you change your mind, we are still looking for a pair for the Christmas party!" She looks hopeful as she looks between the two of us.

"Yah, *Noelle*. Shouldn't you be in the spirit too? Ho. Ho. Ho." I laugh again, with proper motions.

"Nah. You got enough cheer for both of us, *Elijah*."

"Very well," Mrs. Gayle sighs. She is then stolen from the room to help mitigate a scheduling conflict with another bell ringer. This leaves Trouble and me in the room alone. I raise a brow as she walks over and closes the door, locking it.

"So... You're not going to help me out of this rig?" I pull off the belt, jacket, and am already working myself out of the harness.

"Oh no, *Elijah*," her voice takes a soft tone. It is probably the first time in my life I have ever liked my name. She approaches me and helps me out of the flesh bag harness.

The way my back aches after thirty minutes I owe every pregnant woman an apology. I give her a questioning look as she then removes the beard and hair, returning the hat to my head.

"Don't lose your hat, Santa Wolfe," she purrs in my ear as she nips it. I watch as she sinks to her knees, pulling my pants with her.

I am instantly hard as I realize she is going to give me a very merry Christmas present indeed. "Awoo," I grunt once I make this realization.

"Awoo," her warm breath against me followed by the sweet

sensation of her lips surrounding my head nearly brings an early finish to the event. I grip the table I am leaning against and stare at her in awe. There is a unique popping sound as she pulls off. "Laugh for me, Santa," she coos before she quickly draws me to the back of her throat.

"Huh," I strained gasp of a noise that in no way resembles 'ho ho ho' and her chuckling with me in her mouth only makes it worse. "Fuck," I gasp.

She pops off again, and her hand curls around my shaft, gently stroking to give me no reprieve. "Now, now, Santa *Elijah*. No laugh. No finish. Better hurry before she comes back." She gives me a devilish grin.

For the second time today, I have liked someone using my proper name. But damn it all if I am not going to finish. I dig deep, real deep. My hand grabs hold of that ponytail and pulls her back on me as I let out a joyful noise. I swear she shudders against me as I blow my load into her dirty mouth.

God, I love this woman.

# CHAPTER NINE
## *Deck The Halls*

My back hurts. My feet hurt. My arm hurts from ringing the sleigh bells. My cheeks hurt from smiling all damn day. To top it all off my nose hurts from the damn cold too. I'm hungry, need to piss, and I swear to God if one more bratty kid asks to tug my beard to make sure it's real, I'm going to Grinch the hell out of this place. My thoughts keep drifting back to Mrs. Gayle's office, which makes it all the worse as I try not to sport wood while playing Santa. I think Trouble did that on purpose. I haven't seen Trouble since she dropped me off, but I know she is nearby. My stint as Santa has given me plenty of time to stew on how to exact my revenge. It will be delicious. What I have come up with is so epic, Trouble won't know what hit her.

"Merry Christmas," I have said for the billionth time today. The ho ho hos have taken their toll on my stomach as well. I admit I thought I was in shape going into this mess. I have since been shown the light and will hit the gym in the morning.

The crowd is dying down as closing time approaches and the sun has been down for at least an hour. I hope this is not for nothing. If this is a bust, Elle's ass is on the line. I get the feeling the feds won't care too much about it, but I know it will bug her. She has too much to prove to let this case fall apart. I smile thinking about her again. She is nothing like the little girl I remember. That girl had been a weird kid with braces. This woman is confident and sexy as hell. Great, now I am thinking about just how sexy she is and even with the buffer of the Santa suit I'm uncomfortable. I shift my weight to ease the stiffness.

The first blow hits me on the back of my head, and it sends me sprawling forward. I knock the tripod with the bucket to the side as I turn to reach out and grab my assailant. Another fist connects with my jaw, and I grunt. This guy knows how to box. My Santa hat and hair come flying off, leaving the beard askew. He tries to get around me, but I throw a right jab into his gut, knocking the wind out of him. My ears are ringing and the adrenalin's pumping hard enough I'm not thinking on all cylinders, which is why I fail to identify myself as a police officer. I smirk when his fist collides with my Santa stomach. Did this guy really think I was that fat?

His eyes widen as I clock his jaw with my left fist, followed by another jab with the right. Staggering back, he realizes his mistake too late. I can see him weighing the pros and cons of fleeing. I rip off the beard just in time for him to throw himself at me. We collide with the ground, and he pummels me. I fight dirty though and throw a knee to kick him in the ass and send him reeling forward. I use the opportunity to smash my forehead into his nose.

Now I'm pissed at this guy. Not for attacking me but what kind of asshole attacks Santa?

I tried to take my newfound advantage and roll us. Only to

be thwarted by the off-kilter fat-suit. I feel like a damn turtle on the ground as I have to punch up into him without throwing my weight behind the blows. I make do. This fool was decent enough at fighting, but the blow to his nose dazed him. I am known for being hard-headed.

I did not hear the sirens and people shouting as I punch him. I had the size on him and the strength, even if he did get the jump on me. I finally land the blow that counts. I see his eyes roll and then it's lights out for this Grinch. I am panting, and bleeding, as I shove the dead weight off me, using him as the leverage to roll over with him.

"Fuck," I mutter. Looks like I'm going to break all the captain's rules on this case. I quickly reach down to make sure he still has a pulse and I try to start to administer help when I felt hands pulling me away. I balled my fists and was getting ready to swing when I hear her voice.

"Easy, Wolfe. I got you," Elle says. She's being gentle but I barely hear her because my ears are still ringing and I haven't come down from the high of fighting yet so I am dazed. I did not get a chance to reply as I am being handed off to an EMT. He guides me to the ambulance and has me take a seat while he begins the assessment of my injuries.

"Make sure both of them are taken to County General," I hear Agent Harris bark. "Don't forget Santa's bucket. You," she points to a young KCPD officer, "gather these people up and start questioning them on what they saw. Be sure to get their contact information in case there are any further questions." Any hint of the mischievous Elle is gone as she takes control of the scene.

"Joe, look at me," as the EMT shines his penlight in my eyes.

"Would you cut that shit out? I'm fine, Walker." I growl at

him, trying to get a look at Elle, and wanting to get her take on what happened.

"You're not fine, Wolfe. Now, you can get your ass up there on your own, or I can strap you down. Your choice."

I snap my gaze back to him and it does make my head swim a little, but I wasn't going to give him the satisfaction of knowing that. "That's what your sister said," I flash him a grin and I am pretty sure if he was not working, he would have decked me. I then comply and make my way up onto the bus to relax on the stretcher.

It's nearly sunrise when I come strolling out of the emergency room entrance.

"You got one hell of a right jab, kid. Where'd you learn to fight like that?" The man leaning against the brick wall says without removing the cigarette from between his lips.

I cock a brow, and my hackles go up. I'm thankful I didn't have my badge, or gun, on me. My arms are full of the Santa belly and jacket, but I turn to face this guy. "My old man, what's it to you?"

"Easy, slugger. Just here to see if you want to make some extra cash." The guy holds his hands up before he takes the cigarette from his mouth and tosses it to the ground to snuff it out.

"What do you mean, extra cash?"

"Well, I don't think I have seen you on the Santa circuit before."

"Really, you know *every* Santa?"

"Oh, only the ones that know how to deliver. And when it comes to this line of work, we don't look kindly on scabs."

"Scab?" I sound aghast. "What do you mean? This is some kind of union gig? I thought it was all volunteer."

"Well, maybe the suit is. But the people behind the suit," he then clicks his tongue at me as if I should know better. "But I'll have to say, you impressed me, boy. You fight that good all the time?"

"Heh. I have my moments," I smirk.

"Well, if you ever think you might have another one of those moments..." He flicks up a business card like he's performing a magic trick. "Don't forget to call your local representative."

I take the card and watch as he walks away. The damn thing is a blank piece of paper with a handwritten phone number.

This just got interesting.

I make sure he is gone before I saunter to the pay phone on the wall and fish out the coins needed to call the precinct. It takes a few rings before someone picks up in the bullpen.

"Detective Cleaver."

"Cleaver, put Harris on."

"That fine piece of ass ain't here. Try again."

"Where the fuck is she? We caught the perp, right?"

"What? She didn't tell you?" I hear Cleaver laughing on the other end. I roll my eyes as I wait for him to explain. "She took your perp and made it a federal collar. You're out, Wolfe."

"I'm not out, asshole. Get your lazy ass up and go over to my desk. Her card's there. I need her number."

"Hatchett! Go get that skirt's number off Wolfe's desk. He's sniffin' for it." I roll my eyes again. It takes a few minutes, then Cleaver rattles off the number. I don't even thank him as I hang up and fish out the coins I need for the next call.

"Agent Harris speaking," I hear her voice on the line.

"I need an identity."

"Wolfe?"

"Were you expecting somebody else? So can you get me one or not?"

"Why do you need an identity?"

"Things got interesting when I left the hospital. Just trust me on this one, okay? I'll explain when you bring it to me."

"You do realize I am not your golden goose, right? Identities take time and paperwork and reasons, Joe."

"I was approached outside the hospital. Man claimed he was a union representative who apparently represents the men behind the Santas and was mildly impressed with my bell-ringing skills."

"Let me see if the nerds are in yet. Don't hold your breath. Besides, I know the doc said you weren't allowed to do any hard thinkin' for a few days."

"Eh. What do docs know anyway? So, my place, tonight?" I hear her chuckle on the other end.

"Whatever you say, Wolfe. Can I get back to work now?"

"Well, yah. 'Cause I gotta go take a nap." I hang up to make sure I got the last word. I wander back in to the desk and have them hail me a cab to get home.

# CHAPTER TEN
## *Bad Santa!*

I got home and dropped the fat bag on the couch with the jacket. I'm leaning against the fridge trying to figure out if I want a sandwich or a beer when I hear the apartment door open and the tick of my roommate's stilettos as she gets home from the club.

"You hungry?" I call to her.

"Nah. Had breakfast with the girls. Who gave you that shiner? I thought detectives worked a desk?"

"Some asshole who thought he could take on Santa."

"That explains the pants," and then eyes the couch. "Jacket too, huh? Aren't you a little skinny to be playing Santa?"

I decide to fish out a beer, forgetting about the sandwich. "Eh, that's what that flesh-colored torture device is for." I motion to the fat bag. Then chuckle as she ticks into the kitchen and plucks the beer out of my hand. I shake my head and fish out another one for myself.

"Santa, huh?" She looks me over again. "If I'm a good girl, do I get to ride the North pole?"

"Depends," I smirk. "You been a good girl?" I can't help

myself. Meg's not as hot as Elle, but boy can those tits knock a man out. Not to mention she has long legs and a tiny waist. I met Meg a few years ago when I felt the need to head on down to the Brass Pony after a rough night on the beat. Lucky me. Her boyfriend at the time had the same idea. He put hands on her and then I put hands on him. Afterwards, it turns out, the girl needed a safe place to stay, and I was perfectly okay to split the rent with someone. We laid down the ground rules. She doesn't bring guys here. Pays her half of the rent. Keeps herself clean. I make sure she's safe. She became my best friend, even giving me advice on how to woo the girl I was sweet on.

A few months ago, that girl I was sweet on was murdered. That case, and me solving it as a beat cop, is what got me my detective shield. I found solace in Meg's arms. Turns out, she wasn't looking for anything real, but knew I needed to work out my residual anger. Then she said the magic words, no strings attached. We've been roommates with benefits ever since. I take a sip of my beer, eying her as she bites her lip, trying to be cute in asking me for sex. What is it about the Santa suit that makes women frisky? I'm never looking at Santa the same way. I cock an eyebrow as I take in the skimpy dress and body glitter.

"Want me to put the jacket on?" I try not to laugh as she skips to the couch to pick up the jacket. She then gingerly puts the jacket back down and surreptitiously wipes off her hand as she comes back to me.

"Uh, maybe next time."

I start to ask her why, then she draws me into a kiss, pressing her body against mine. I'll figure it out later.

Her well-manicured nails trail down my stomach pushing

the suspenders aside to allow the pants to pool at my knees. I set my beer down and reach behind her, unfastening her dress just enough to expose those perfect tits. I don't think I have ever seen her in a bra. Her kisses trail down my body until she's able to nestle my hardening cock right between her tits. I was only at half-mast before. But now, with those soft and perky things hugging my cock nice and snug, I was giving her my best salute. She works me up and down, letting her hot tongue tease around the head before I'm reaching down to pull her up and turn her around.

My kitchen is a little galley kitchen, and it's cramped in here. But I didn't want to take the time to head into her room, or the living room. I flip that piece of fabric up and push her thong aside as I thrust into her from behind. One hand on her shoulder while the other holds onto her hip. It's hard and fast. Then I let go of my hold to cup those magnificent breasts. She arches back to me as I knead her soft skin, and I pinch those already taught nipples roughly. Her hips work in a perfect circular motion as she impales herself on my shaft. I have to bite the inside of my mouth to keep from laughing as she moans like a porn star, "Oh Santa! Santa. I've been a naughty girl."

That's my queue to pinch harder and give her nipples little twists. She moans louder and tightens as she rides me. I close my eyes, enjoying the feeling of her body. Slowly, the glittered stripper before me transforms into the sexy as hell woman I had at the Wolfe's Den. I feel my cock twitch at the idea of this being Elle and pump harder. My hands grip tighter, squeezing her breasts together as I near orgasm. I was getting lost in my imagination of Elle when Meg starts her screaming wail of, "Yes! Yes! Yes!"

I could feel her milking me hard as she achieved her climax. I pull out just in time to explode on her ass. The thoughts of Elle dashed from my mind.

She is still as she pants over the counter. "That was... perfect, Santa Joe."

I smirk and give her a proper slap on the ass. "Merry Christmas, little Meg. You've been an exceptionally good girl." I step back as she straightens herself up. I pull my own pants up in the process and return the suspenders to my shoulders.

"Goodnight, Joe," she giggles as she walks away, her tits still hanging out. I will never tire of that sight.

I grab my beer and head to my room to turn in myself.

When my eyes flutter open again, Meg is leaning over me. "Joe, wake up. There's someone here to see you. I think I pissed her off."

"Wha? Who?" I'm groggy and disoriented as I try to work through the fog of what Meg just said.

"Joe, c'mon. Get up."

"Yah, *Elijah*. Get up." The bemused voice of Agent Harris cuts through the air as she leans in the doorway.

I cut Trouble a dark look and fuss off Meg. "Yah. Give me a minute. I'm workin' on it. You need to give a man a moment to wake up." I rub my hand over my face as I throw back the covers to crawl out of bed. I see the exchange of looks between Meg and Trouble. Meg looks nervous and Trouble, well, the name suits her. I am grateful she turns to follow Meg instead of harassing me further. I am fairly sure I saw water in her hand. I wouldn't put it past her to dump it on my head to speed me up. Doesn't take me long to pull on boxers and a T-Shirt before I come walking out.

Meg's grin tells me she is stirring this pot. "I got it from here, Meg. Thanks for seeing her in." I swear these women are trying to kill me.

She saunters right up and kisses my cheek before wandering back to her room. "Anytime, Santa Joe." I did not expect that and am staring at Meg as she walks away. Then Agent Harris clears her throat.

"Sorry about that," I mutter as I run my fingers through my disheveled hair.

"Wolfe, what you do on your time, is your business. The identity you asked for."

I see it in her eyes, the spark of jealousy. I was about to make a crack about how she could join the two of us, but thought better of it. Instead, I take the envelope and plop down in my chair in the living room. She shoves her hands in her pockets and leans against the arm of the couch as I proceed to tell her all about my new friend. "With how shady he was, that's why I called you. I figured if I was going to go down this rabbit hole, I needed to be Alice, not Joe."

"Great. Anything else, Wolfe?"

"What? You're not gonna tell me anything else you found out about the perp we pulled in?"

"Don't know. You seem awfully busy. Hate to take away from Meg time." There's that spark again.

I roll my eyes and correct her. "She's my roommate."

"Uh, huh. Great. I don't discuss cases with roommates."

"Well, you're not discussing cases with her. You're discussing it with me." I frown at her. "Your partner."

"Informant," she taunts back at me.

"Okay. When did I get demoted?" I see the gears turning, as she does not immediately respond to me. When she starts to speak, I cut her off, expecting the canned FBI 'we're taking your shit' response. "Really? You're cutting me out just because I'm KCPD? I thought you were different from the average fed."

"You know what, Joe," she starts in a heated tone, then stops. It's like she decided to change what she was going to say mid thought. Her expression goes from irritated, to the stone cold poker face, and she frowns. Her tone is even when she speaks again. "Go over your identity and make sure it's right. I'll talk to you in a few days when I have the information you asked for." Her response makes me grimace as I literally watch her shut off all emotion to speak with me. Before I can respond, she turns her back to me and leaves. She almost sells she isn't angry, but the door slamming on her way out told me otherwise.

"You really are an idiot," I hear Meg say as she comes out of her room.

"What did I do this time?" I feel like they're teaming up against me.

"Really, Joe? I thought you said she was your partner. You yell at all your partners like that?"

"I wasn't yelling," I yell at Meg.

"Uh, huh. And do you tell your partners they are just an asshole fed out to screw you over? I mean. She made a trip over here to give you that and you didn't even look at it."

"Hmph," I now understand why women make this noise.

This brings a laugh out of Meg as she sits down on the couch. "She's a looker. Bent her over a chair yet?" She flashes me a devious grin. I can't help myself, and I blush in response. "You dog! Here?"

I just shake my head, trying to ignore her.

"You like her." Meg accuses me.

"She's good at her job."

"Uh. Huh. And that job is…"

"Being a damn good cop."

"So, then why did you tear her down?" Damn women and their sneaky logic. How did we get back to this question?

"I didn't…" I squeak. "Fuck," I mutter in response to her cocked eyebrow, as I realize I have unjustifiably torn into Elle for a second time. I owe her another fritter, and an apology. I'm beginning to make a habit of being an ass to her. I sigh and surrender to this interrogation. If women are always this good at tearing down defenses, why aren't we leveraging this power more?

"Ask her to dinner. And flowers. I bet she likes flowers. And every girl likes chocolate. Ooh. You could send her one of those chocolate gram things to where she works."

"There is no way in hell, I am sending a candy gram to the FBI. That would only make it worse. She's trying hard enough to not be viewed as just a skirt. I am definitely not going to embarrass her that way."

Meg gives me a sideways glance, "Good to know, you're not just easy to look at. You've got some kind of smarts in there. So. Where did you bend her over?"

I chuckle and leave the conversation at that as I hop up out of the chair. As I head back to my room, "If you want to know that, you'll have to join in."

I stumble as she responds with, "I always have had a thing for brunettes."

# CHAPTER ELEVEN
## *You're A Mean One, Mr. Wolfe*

The phone rings and I am in the shower, mid rinse.

"Meg," I call. The phone keeps ringing.

"Meg!" Now I have shampoo in my eyes. The phone is still ringing.

"Fuck!" I quickly get rinsed and kill the shower. The ringing stops when I reach the phone on my nightstand. I glare at the phone like it had done it on purpose, then turn to finish getting dried off in the bathroom. The phone rings again as soon as I reach for the comb.

"Hello," I growl into the phone.

"Don't get snippy with me, boy. You're the one that didn't pick up the damn phone," my uncle Jerry barks at me.

"What do you want old man? I'm busy."

"I found a lost pup for you to pick up."

"I'm not in the habit of pickin' up strays. Call 'em a cab?"

"I think you're gonna want to do this one yourself, kid. Trust me."

"Fine. Fine. I'll be there." We hang up and I furrow my brow. I rack my brain trying to figure out why he thinks I would want to pick up this stray. I shake my head and finish getting dressed. It only takes me twenty minutes before I am walking into the Wolfe's Den. A quick survey of the room does not reveal this mystery stray to me. Then I hear her.

"Heaver... Why don't I lose your Catchett for you! I have real work police to do."

"Uh huh, sure you do, Agent Harris. How many have you had, honey?"

"Not my honey! Enough!"

I hesitate, watching the scene unfold. While it is hilarious that she is running circles around those two in such a drunken state, it worries me that she is in such a state. My uncle sees me lingering in the door and motions to her. I give him a nod and begin my approach.

"C'mon, sweetheart. We'll take you home." Hatchett reaches for Elle's forearm. I'm not sure how she does it, but Hatchett is now on the floor and her drink is still in hand.

"No!" she sounds like a petulant child. "My touch!"

Cleaver helps Hatchett up off the floor, but I can see the pissed off look on the man from here. I decide this is the perfect opportunity for my superhero moment. "Hatchett, you never did learn to keep your hands to yourself. When a lady says no, she means no." I step between Elle and the other detectives.

"You don't need me to fight, dog!" She shouts at me from behind. I wish I was recording this somehow. Cleaver and I exchange a glance and the two of them wander off. This allows me to turn around and face my damsel.

"No, I don't," I grin. "But I think maybe we should go get a cup of coffee before those knuckleheads try anything else." Up close, I can see the disheveled look.

"No!" She tries to take a step back and gets trapped by the bar. I step forward, crowding her in. "Mine," she hoards the drink to her.

"All yours, just going to get it refilled," I gently reach to take it from her hand and watch as her eyes narrow up at me. I hold my hand up, "Scout's honor. It's just a refill."

"Tequilla!" She slurs.

"I'll see what I can manage," as I get the glass from her. I wander behind the bar and come back with a glass of water.

"Sat not tequilla. Liar dirty." She brandishes a finger in my general direction. Any amusement at the situation is gone, as I can see she is well beyond the limit. Why would my uncle keep serving her?

"I said a refill. You drink this, and then we'll talk Tequilla." I hold the glass up tantalizingly.

"Drink? Then Tequilla?"

I nod. She snatches the drink from my hand and throws it back, like a tequila shot and shoves the glass back in my hand, motioning for the promised tequila. Then her eyes go wide, and her hands cover her mouth. I recognize the universal motion of getting ready to pray to the porcelain gods. I shift my weight to allow her a direct path and turn her in the right direction.

She barrels into the women's restroom, slams into the stall and drops to her knees. I barely catch up in time to get a hand around her ponytail and pull it clear as the tequila is offered as tribute. Three heaving rounds later, she is panting, exhausted from her efforts. Her arms rest on the seat and her forehead on her arms. I step back and fill the glass with water, then offer it to her.

"Away you go, Wolfe," she whines against the toilet.

"Not yet. Come on, take a few swigs of that." I step out of the stall to give her a moment. I lean against the sink and cross my arms as she gargles and spits out the water. I watch as she precariously picks herself up and stumbles out of the stall, looking like death warmed over.

"Not being here good," she furrows her brow at me.

I chuckle softly and nod. "Yes, not being here is good. C'mon." I guide her out. The drunken path to the door could be categorized as the serpentine motion. Once outside, I put her in the passenger seat of my car and buckle her in. The drive back to my apartment is chilly as she rolled down the window and hung her head out like a lost puppy. She is out cold by the time I pull into my parking lot. With some effort, I scoop her up and carry her into my apartment.

I drop my keys on the table and carry her into my bedroom to gently set her on the bed. I slip her shoes off and notice she is still wearing her weapon holster. With a grunt of effort from shifting her dead weight, I wrangle her suit jacket off of her, followed by the harness. Then I shift her up the bed to put her head on the pillow and pull the covers over her. I had slept most of the day, so now it is time to sit down and actually read through all the paperwork she gave me before she stole my case.

With a cup of coffee in hand, I sit at the table and dump the contents of the envelope out. The contents are impressive, my whole new life laid bare. Those FBI nerds definitely know how to put the bow on the package. How the hell did she get this so fast? It takes weeks for anything from the nerds at KCPD, and that's with bribery. I study my new driver's license and grimace as they somehow found a worse picture than the one on my actual license. I sift through information about bank accounts, credit accounts, and take a moment to study the faces of the smiling people in all my wallet-sized pictures. They even gave me a gently used leather wallet to hold all my goodies. I hate to admit that I'm impressed. I spend the rest of the evening hours memorizing the dossier given to me about my new identity.

I had drifted to sleep on the couch at some point when Meg comes walking in. The tick of her heels wakes me, but I don't open my eyes. I smile when she drapes one of Grandma Wolfe's quilts over me, but I don't otherwise engage with her. Meg's long asleep when I hear a groan from my bedroom. Trouble must be stirring. With a chuckle, I get up and head into the kitchen to cook. I glance at the clock, and it is near noon. Probably a good thing it's Saturday.

"Mornin', Elle. I made you breakfast," I smile at her when she finally comes stumbling in. I set a plate full of scrambled eggs, bacon, and sausage down in front of her, along with a bottle of aspirin and a glass of orange juice.

"Why am I at your place, Wolfe?" she groans.

"Because I would have had to touch inappropriate places to find the keys to your place."

"You weren't at the bar."

"You're right. I wasn't at the bar. The old man turned on the bat signal and here we are. Now eat. While it's still hot."

She gives me a dubious look but obeys and eats her breakfast.

I wait until the dishes are done before I strike up the conversation again. "I looked over the file you gave me. Damn good work."

She rubs her hand over her face and watches me with that poker face of hers. "Good. Probably not wise to show up around the Wolfe's Den much while working that. I'll be your point of contact, and we'll meet only when it's safe." She is all business, and none of the banter we had before yesterday.

I watch her as I refill her orange juice. "This is probably the only time you are ever going to hear these words from me, so savor it." I take a deep breath dramatically. "I… owe you… an apology. Sorry. I was a dick. The stuff you got me is perfect for the undercover work I need to be doing. You didn't deserve for me to snap at you like that, and I should have waited for you to finish explaining. So, want to tell me about last night?"

I watch as her eyes go as wide as silver dollars at my apology. She says nothing in response and watches me like an owl watching a field mouse. She then sets her orange juice down and I see the gears turning again. She is deciding how much to let me in. I learned my lesson from yesterday and patiently wait for her to say something.

"My boss wants you off the case. But you are the case. Without your work, we have nothing. So… I broke the rules, and he made your captain look like a pussycat with how pissed he was. But agreed, so long as you were an informant, not a partner." She pauses to take a sip of her orange juice, "Then, my douche bag partner decided to get his dick bent out of shape even when I did what he asked." She gives me a wry grin. "But the truth is. I was in that bar, hoping to fuck the first pretty thing that walked in and pretend I'm not a Harris for the night."

I clear my throat, "What does being a Harris have to do with anything?"

She gives me a look; one I have seen on Maman's face before. It's that look that says I am being dumb and should know the answer. Why do women do that? I don't reply, because if I knew the answer I wouldn't have asked the question.

"Skip met me at the gym and informed that under no circumstances was I to miss their annual ball for St. Jude. And, as if I don't have enough shit wrangling a Wolfe, I am to 'engage'," she air quotes, "with all the eligible young men my mother has lined up. So my parents can decide the best match for me to not have to continue this phase of being an agent."

I can't help myself, I laugh. "So, you're gonna just what? Skip it? Seems like a perfectly reasonable thing to do in my opinion."

She gives me a pointed look, "You're telling me you are going to skip Christmas with the Wolfe family?"

"Ah. Touché. So, what are you going to do about it?"

"Show up engaged." She gives me a smirk. I have a bad feeling about this, but I have to ask.

"Engaged, to whom?"

She bats her eyelashes at me. I knew this girl was going to be Trouble.

## CHAPTER TWELVE

### God Rest Ye Merry Gentlemen

"Why do I have to wear this monkey suit again?" I tug at the tie for the tenth time in as many minutes. Then she puts it back for the tenth time in as many minutes.

"Because, *my love*," she emphasizes the words with an amused smirk, "you want to impress my snobby, well-to-do parents. Not to mention the police commissioner will be in attendance."

"Okay, lady. You need to be careful with that big L word. You could shatter a fragile man's heart throwing it around casually." I have a mock serious expression on my face.

"Elijah Wolfe, I never pegged you for such a romantic." She winks at me, then pinches my cheek.

"Hmph!" I give her a taste of her own medicine. Of course, she is distracting as hell right now in that tiny slip of black fabric she calls a dress.

"Didn't your mother specifically ask you to wear something Christmasy?"

"Mhm hmm," she smiles.

I groan, "Well, I guess if we're doing this..."

"Awe, C'mon Wolfe. We'll be in and out in thirty minutes, tops. We'll get in, find my parents, break the news, and run. Then I'll concoct our fabulous break-up a few days later. Enjoy the open bar."

"Nuh uh. Nope. No alcohol is getting anywhere near this tux. Do you know how much of a deposit I had to put on this thing? There is no way in hell, I am getting barf near this."

I swear I see the devil come out of her in the grin she gives me. She steps in close and whispers, "Guess that means no coat closet," before she turns to start up the stairs.

"You play dirty. You know that!"

"I don't know what you mean, *my love.*" Then she has the gall to do the cutest thing ever. She calls to me in a sweet tone, "Awoo?"

"Awoo." I grunt in confirmation. "Remember, you owe me for this. And you said anything." I then plaster a formal smile on my face as I catch up to her and we breach the inner sanctum of this party.

She laughs and takes my arm with ease. I can't help but smile at her. It may be entirely fake, our engagement, but having her on my arm is not such a terrible thing. This party is a who's who of Kansas City. The commissioner, the fire chief, the deputy mayor, a bunch of young schmucks in tuxes, and their old, rich fathers. Trouble wasn't joking about the dog and pony show of suitors her parents were foisting upon her. There is champagne and what I can only assume to be Caviar. At least, that's what I hope those weird little black pellets are. We make our way through the room, talking and laughing appropriately. This woman even steals kisses on my cheek as other people fawn over us.

"You look lovely this evening, Miss Harris. Who is your

handsome young friend?" The man before us, stands about the same height as me. His face is clean shaved, but he could easily grow a beard. His dark hair combed back, and the way he smiles at Elle, gives me the used-car salesman vibe. I instinctively ease closer to her, staking my claim.

"Mr. Kleinfeld, you look dashing this evening, as always. This is, uh... My... Joe. Joe Wolfe." I chuckle at her bit of awkwardness as I hold out my hand to shake.

"Pleasure to meet you, Mr. Kleinfeld." His handshake is firm, and that's when it finally clicks where I know that name from. The man standing before us, is Atticus Kleinfeld. He is one of the best money men in Kansas City. More than half this town was built with money from the Kleinfeld family's bank.

"Are you one of John's kids?"

"Yes, sir. Born and raised. Lucky number seven."

"Your father's a good man. I voted for him when he was in Congress. I like what he did for Missouri."

"I'm sure he appreciated your vote," I give my canned response, as most people don't realize I am too young for his politicking days. I was technically born in Washington D.C. while my father represented the state. But we moved back a year later when my mother died giving birth to Hope-Marie. We exchange a few more pleasantries with the man, and he bemoans his son not catching Trouble's attention. It reminds me just how flush her parents are. While my parents have money, they made sure we grew up with our own healthy work ethic. I would need to have a damn good reason before I would even think about asking them for a dime. I admit, I enjoy peacocking around with Trouble in front of all these spoiled silver spoon babies. Even if it's fake, she's all mine tonight.

Trouble was leading us to the bar when we get ambushed.

"You didn't tell me your mystery guy is Joe Wolfe, Elle." I heave a heavy sigh as I turn to face Skip Harris, my former best friend. We stare each other down. I notice Elle shift a little uncomfortably next to me. Then Skip and I break into grins, clap hands, and pull each other into a one-armed hug. We give a hardy slap on the back before breaking apart.

"How the hell you been, man? It's been what, ten years since we last saw each other?" I knew exactly how long it had been since we had a falling out.

"Yah, something like that. Ever since you stole my girl junior year." Apparently, he did too.

"It's not my fault she wanted a Wolfe." I mock innocence and see Trouble roll her eyes.

"She didn't. She wanted me and you seduced her. Eh. I can't be too mad, though. You did save me from a fate worse than death."

"Do I want to know?"

"Two words. Gold. Digger. I think she's on husband number four."

"Whew. Well, she was fucking hot."

"Great. If you two are done with this circle jerk, maybe we should go tell mom and pop the good news?" I swear she wriggled her brows at me, knowing she was about to rile her brother up.

"What good news?" His tone darkens as he stares at me.

"She's not pregnant, man. I can tell you that much."

"Wait. That was an option?" Skip's face is turning redder by the second. Then he looks at his sister and his expression turns murderous when she does not diffuse the situation.

"Oh, come off it, Skip. You knew I was fucking Wolfe from our conversation the other day."

"Yah. But there's a difference between fucking and maybe having his fucking baby."

"They'd be cute babies," I hear the words leaving my mouth before my brain registered what I was putting out in the universe.

Both Harris siblings stop and stare at me. I am fairly sure Skip is going to punch me, so I prepare myself to take the blow like a man. It's Trouble's expression that makes me smirk. Her eyes are wide as saucers in surprise that I would even suggest we are having children together. Thankfully, the punch never comes.

"Who is having cute babies? Is there something you want to tell me, Charles? Amanda?" Mrs. Harris, Mr. Harris, and who I can only assume to be the effervescent Mandy appear.

Skip coughs and sputters as the dyed platinum blond comes over to take his arm. "Charlie, what is she talking about?"

"Yah, *Charlie*," Trouble teases his name like she does me when she is living up to her name.

"What is that on your finger?" Mrs. Harris snatches Trouble's hand and yanks it forward into the little circle that has formed. There, sparkling on her ring finger, is a gold band with diamonds. Where the hell did she get a ring like that? My eyes are glued to the sparkling piece of jewelry as I try to process the fact she has a ring on. One, I supposedly gave to her.

"Oh, I meant to tell you—"

"It's stunning!" Mandy cuts in and squeals with delight. "I can't wait for Charlie to buy me a ring."

"Yah, *Skip*, when are you going to buy a ring?" I try to change the topic.

"Who's Skip?" This makes Trouble and I shoot each other a devilish grin, like she's telling me *I told you so*. Poor Charlie. He's standing there with his mouth opening and closing like a fish out of water. He is still trying to catch up with how the tables have turned from his sister's mystery ring to the lack of a ring of his own.

Mrs. Harris does not allow us to weasel out of the conversation. She is much too sharp for that as she has not released Trouble's hand. "What is the meaning of this, Noelle Winifred Harris?"

I try to hold back my amusement, but the snort escapes me, drawing daggers from Mrs. Harris. I definitely tuck that information away for future reference. Then Mrs. Harris turns her motherly wrath on me.

"Elijah Joseph Wolfe. Just what do you find funny, young man?" That's it, we're dead. She just used my full name, too. Here, I thought maybe she didn't recognize me.

"Well, mother," Trouble yanks her hand free and then has the balls to tuck it into the crook of *my* arm. "That's what I came here to tell you tonight." It sounds chipper and confident enough to the casual onlooker, but I hear the small squeak in Trouble's voice as she alludes to the fact we are engaged.

"Noelle," the deep voice of her father cuts across all the antics in our little circle. I watch with dread to see if Trouble has the balls to outright lie to her parents about being engaged. It's one thing to talk about it. It's another to look your parents in the eyes and tell them a straight up lie.

"We're really happy, Pop," she goes from Trouble to Noelle, the perfect daughter, in no time flat. This girl needs a fucking

Oscar for this performance. I watch as she expertly weaves our tale without actually saying we are engaged. Until Mandy, the one person we never expected, drops the bomb on us.

"So, how did he propose?" Her doe-like eyes filled with proverbial hearts as she wants to hear the absolute most romantic thing possible. It is clear she wants Charlie to take notes.

I have a bad feeling about this when Trouble turns and smiles up at me. I thought for sure she would pin the story telling on me. Then she opens her mouth again. "It was so sweet. Joe here, is a hopeless romantic," she teases. "We were on an assignment together between our divisions and spent a lot of time cramped in a car. Then, the perp got the jump on me in a chase. And Joe here, he was my knight in shining armor. Came rushing in all fists and badge, scooped me right up and carried me to safety. Next thing I knew, he was on one knee asking me to be his partner, forever."

Mandy hangs on every word, swooning with Trouble's tale. I am not too concerned with her. Instead, I am watching Mr. Harris. The old man's eyes darken with every word that comes out of Trouble's mouth. "You're marrying a cop?" His voice booms across the room, silencing the crowd. "I forbid it." The edict comes down from Zeus on high and I swear I see Trouble grin.

On cue, the waterworks spring forth from my lovely fiancée. "But I love him!" she shouts back at him before turning and bolting out of the room in all the dramatic flair. I am stunned as again, she uses the L word. Then I realize she left me here.

"Uh. Excuse me. I should... go... after her," as I also bolt out of the room. I realize this was her entire exit strategy when I finally reach the car, and she's leaning against it, grinning like a hyena.

"Awoo!" She crows my own damn callsign to me.

"Nuh uh. No. Not Awoo!" I pause trying to decide if tonight's shenaniganry lives up to an awoo status. "Okay. Maybe just a little Awoo." I wink at her as I get in the driver seat.

She then, in the most adorable way possible, chirps, "Awoo!" As she slides into the passenger seat.

# CHAPTER THIRTEEN
## *Naughty or Nice?*

"Joe," I hear Meg call through my door with a knock.

I crack an eye open and glance at the alarm clock on my nightstand. I groan and ignore her. If she just wants attention, she'll have to come back later. It's too early for anything after last night with Trouble. Every muscle in my body is sore. Even the extra-long, hot shower when I got home didn't ease that ache.

"Joe," Meg's voice grows more impatient, "look. We agreed to not bring strays back here, and this is the second one you have brought home."

That gets my attention, and I sit up. Who the fuck could be out there? It wouldn't be Agent Harris, as we agreed it would be bad to be seen coming and going from each other's place now that I'm Erik Thatcher. The girlfriend in my file doesn't really exist, and none of Meg's friends are on the can-do list. I grumble as I push off the bed and stalk to my door, jerking it open. I see Meg smirking at me before she turns to head to her room. She just got off work and is still covered in glitter.

"Joseph," I hear Maman's soft French accent. "Put some clothes on before you embarrass yourself." She is being reproachful but is chuckling.

I turn pink and cover myself, closing the bedroom door again. Fuck, these women are going to be the death of me. I quickly pull on boxers and pants, followed by a T-shirt. Seconds later, I am coming back out to the main room, closing my bedroom door behind me. I didn't want Maman to see I needed to pick up in there. I swoop in and wrap her into a tight hug, spinning her. It's kind of our thing. "What brings you here this early in the morning? You want some coffee?"

"Oui," she starts with the coffee and that tells me I'm in trouble. I give her a side glance as I step into the narrow galley kitchen and fire up my old Mr. Coffee machine. The tiny French woman that has raised me since I was a year old was not a woman to be trifled with. I am quite sure she could kill someone in their sleep the way she looks when crossed. She's a bombshell and is probably the reason for my fascination with blonds. Her naturally blond hair, which has started to turn platinum, is always curled and styled to perfection. Her eyes are the most piercing green you have ever seen, and she accents that feature with the cherry red lipstick that is never smeared. At sixty years old, she is one of the most beautiful women I have ever laid eyes on.

"You want any breakfast?"

"Non, I have already eaten, Joseph. I came by to offer my congratulations, and to help you plan the announcement party, then to plan the ceremony. Based on the suddenness, I can only assume zhat you are about to make your father a proud grandfather."

There it is, the dagger in me. Fuck, she thinks I am engaged and Elle pregnant. "Ma, it's complicated."

"How is it complicated? You proposed. She said yes. All

zhat is left to do is get married, ne c'est pas?" She cocks her head and I feel like I am sitting under the interrogation lights at the precinct.

"Well… I didn't propose," I turn my attention to scooping the coffee grounds into the filter instead of looking her in the eyes.

"Oh, so she proposed to you, and you said yes, just like your sister. It makes no difference which one proposed." I chuckle at the thickness of her French accent right now. She has not lived in France for thirty years and can sound as American as the rest of us. She is doing it on purpose to force me to pay attention to her. While I don't speak it often, my siblings and I are fluent in French. It came in real handy in high school with the girls. As if she could read my mind, she switches over to French, "How far along is she?"

I choke.

"Maman! No! Nuh uh. Not pregnant. Nothing like that. Look," I run my hand through my hair. Fuck, this is getting worse. I can't lie to this woman. She always sees right through it. I am pretty convinced if she weren't so young, she would have been a spy for The Resistance in France back during World War II. I narrow my eyes at her and grunt.

"Joseph Wolfe, you are not lying to zhat girl's parents, are you? You know it would disappoint your father if you were doing something deceitful like that."

"Dad knows?" I whine and pour the filled pot of water into the machine before settling it on the hot plate and turning on the switch. The little machine bubbles to life and begins gurgling as it sucks up the water. I stare at the brewing coffee like it's the most interesting thing in the world before I finally move to the entryway and lean against it. My arms are crossed in front of me, and I frown at Maman. I promised Trouble I would keep the facade up until she either told her parents the truth, or we mysteriously broke up. But this is my parents we're talking about, and I did not expect news to travel back to them. I don't lie to my parents. So, I evade like a dog fighter in aerial combat.

"He was so excited this morning when Mr. Harris told him the news." She gives me a smile then, and I knew I had been made. The mischievous glint in her eye reminded me of the look on Trouble's face when I escaped the party last night. "So, when would you like your engagement party?"

"Ma, I can't even think about that right now. I have to get done with this case first."

"Fair enough," she sulks and makes me feel like an even bigger jerk. The coffee finishes brewing, and I bring her a mug. I listen to her antics the few minutes she takes to sip the coffee, but then she has to leave to get to school on time. She is the high school's French and German teacher, and I am pretty convinced she knows we aren't engaged. I rub my hand over my face after she is gone and have half a mind to wake Trouble up.

As if I had summoned the devil herself, my phone rings. "Yah?" I don't answer the phone with the correct greeting since I'm not supposed to be Joe Wolfe right now. Maman would box my ears for being so rude.

"Good morning," Trouble's voice chirps on the other end. "Just calling to remind you to return the Santa suit today. I would hate to have to bail Mrs. Gayle out due to violence being committed upon you." I grin at the sarcasm in her tone.

"Yah, about that. It's toast. Do you know where I can find a new one?"

"Yup! You can pick it up at the dry cleaners on Mackenzie after three p.m."

"Cuttin' it close, aren't ya? And... Uh... I guess, thank you?"

"Yah, I saw how you looked when they loaded you on the bus. I called in a favor."

"Appreciate it. So, you remember how you said you would do anything if I performed well?"

"Yeah, but I don't think we should have that kind of sex until the case is over." I smirk as I realize she is probably not opposed to what I was thinking.

"Uhm. While I was originally planning on using it for that, plans change."

"Oh?"

"Yup. My mother showed up on my doorstep this morning, congratulating me on my engagement. So, my anything, is *you* have to tell my mother the truth." Silence is the reply I get. I wait her out, as I can only imagine the gears turning in her head.

"You really want to waste it on that? What if we just break up?"

"Even if we break up," I air quote it even though she can't see me. "You still have to tell her the truth. I want this thing clean slated. No black marks on my scorecard because you needed a favor."

"I don't have to say shit if we break up. We broke up." I hear her chuckling on the other end.

"Hmm. Yah. But the thing about breaking up with me before Christmas, is your mother is likely to pull off a Christmas miracle. I mean, unless you like pretty man-boys with money."

"They're good for three things, pal. Sex, diamonds, and

imported cars. Not for getting married."

"Well, good to know you're not a gold digger." I hear her chuckle again. "You still have to tell Maman. I don't lie to my parents."

"You realize, omission is still lying, right?"

"Nope. I neither confirmed nor denied. There's a difference." I can't believe I just gave her a political-ass answer.

"Uh, huh. I need to get back to work. Let me know what you find and don't forget the suit." She hangs up on me. I'm not sure if she agreed or not, based on that conversation, but I don't have a good feeling about it either way.

"You know, your life is getting better than General Hospital. When the fuck did you get engaged? I thought you were fucking the agent." Meg chirps as she plops down across from me at the table and steals my coffee.

"Okay, you can't tell anyone. Especially not Maman. I have to keep up appearances. Okay?" I realize I sound like a crazy person. There is no reason at all for me to keep up the charade, other than it wins points with Elle. "And, for the record. It is the agent."

"*You* like her," she teases me, and my face has the gall to turn as red as the Santa suit. What the hell is happening to me? I rub my hand over my face.

"No. I mean, yes. I mean, I work with her, and I knew her when we were kids."

"Awe, childhood sweethearts, reunited."

"Well, we weren't sweethearts then. She was just the kid sister with braces. I was friends with her brother."

"Oh. So, ugly duckling with a secret crush!"

"You watch too many soap operas. I am going to nap before I have to go get a Santa suit." I flee from the conversation, as I am not ready to think about anyone like that. I need to focus on this case, and she is my partner, not my girlfriend. If I screw this up, it's more than my ass on the line. But I'll be damned if I wasn't looking forward to the next evening alone with her in the back seat of my car.

# CHAPTER FOURTEEN
## *Sleigh Bells Ring*

I picked up the suit from the cleaners and was in Mrs. Gayle's office with five minutes to spare. I don't know what kind of favor Agent Harris had to call in, but Mrs. Gayle doesn't know it's a new suit. Happy to not have ruined Christmas, I hum along with the carols playing on the radio as I drive to my next destination.

I stop at a convenience store and fish out the business card my "union rep" gave me. I didn't want to use my regular phone number in case they traced it back to me. It also sells the financial hardship my profile shows I have. Gambling and drinking are my vices, plus a girlfriend with champagne tastes.

"Yah?" The voice on the other end growls like I had interrupted him from something important.

"Hey. My union rep said to call him at this number if I was interested in joining." I rub my nose and watch the cars passing by. This pay phone wasn't in a booth, so the chilly wind makes me hunker down in my Carhart jacket as I hear him shout for someone named Miles.

"Miles here, who's this?" The other man casually asks.

"You still offering that job you talked about outside the hospital?"

"Hey, kid. You bet. Stop by The Wooden Nickel and I'll get all your paperwork in order. What's your name again?"

"Thatcher," I say. "See you in a few."

I sigh as I look at the shit brown rental that is my ride for the foreseeable future, making me miss my Firebird already. It only takes me ten minutes to get to the bar, but I lean against my steering wheel staring at the building for a few minutes before I decide to get this show on the road. This building is nondescript and looks like all the other metal boxes that line the street. The only sign that it is a bar at all is the large circular sign made to look like a large buffalo nickel with the words 'The Wooden Nickel' burned into it. I couldn't linger out here too long, as it would look weird, so I hoist myself out of the car to head inside.

Inside is just how I imagined it would be. There are booths along a wall with high backs and black leather. Sprinkled in the middle of the room are a couple of tables that will sit up to four people. Shoved to the opposite of the booths is the bar, with a jukebox tucked near the end. In the corner, are two dart boards with a chalkboard that is gray from the chalk dust. Behind the bar is a bear of a man. I am sure he eats guys like me for breakfast. With his buzz cut hair, broad nose that has definitely been broken, and a flat brow, he reminds me of Lurch, if Lurch were a hulking, heavyweight boxer. At the middle of the bar, sitting on a barstool, is my union rep, Miles.

"Took you long enough, kid. Have a seat." He motions next to him, and I oblige.

"What'll you have?" says Lurch.

"Budweiser," I say without thinking. I reach for my wallet

and Miles waves me off.

"Nah, kid. This one's on me. So, you really want to join the union?" He takes a sip of whatever hard liquor drink he has in his hand.

"Yup. Can't find shit for work, and while the Santa gig's fun and all, I'd rather get paid in cash, not cookies. Girlfriend's bleedin' me dry. Since I got laid off, it has been rough."

"It's not for everyone. What I'm about to show you stays between us, you got it? Word gets out I took on a charity case, and I'll have all these assholes jabbering for a handout."

"Don't need no handout. I'll earn my keep," I growl in response as the bartender hands me a beer. I watch as Miles sizes me up and can see the gears turning in his mind. He's trying to decide if he can trust me.

A look between him and the bartender must have settled the matter as he eases up off the stool and motions, "Come on, kid. Let me show you the ropes."

I follow, bringing my beer with me. I'm not about to pass up free beer. We move toward the jukebox. Both of my brows raise when Miles punches in a couple of keys on the jukebox and the theme from Rocky blasts out of the speakers. I think he is still screwing with me until the wall panel next to the jukebox pops out with a hiss of a noise. This is some weird mechanical cloak and dagger stuff. To have a setup like this, someone has to be funding these guys. I make a mental note to remember the song and follow him into the dimly lit opening.

It leads down a flight of stairs and I can hear the door hissing closed behind us, causing the artificial light to flicker on above us. I am glad I brought the bottle with me, as I have some kind of weapon if I need to fight my way out of here.

I'm watching the back of Miles' head as he approaches another person standing in front of a door.

"Hello, Mr. Santorro! I see you brought a friend today. The buy in is five. Who would you like to pick?" I shift my weight to see around Miles and she is the cutest little number, dressed up just like a Playboy Bunny without the ears and tail. I whistle low and put on the smolder for her, which makes Miles chuckle.

"Keep it in your pants. Unless you want to answer to the guy upstairs. Afternoon, Alicia, I'm entering a new guy today. What did you say your name was again, kid?"

"Thatcher," I say and resist completing the James Bond moment with my first name.

"Wonderful," Alicia chirps and turns to the massive chalk board I hadn't seen before, writing in my last name at the bottom of the list. Miles fills out a little book she is holding, and then motions for me to follow him. "Your usual bet?"

"Yes, ma'am," he smiles at her as he leads me through another door. I notice that he had put five thousand on me to win.

I definitely am surprised when I see what's behind door number two. It's an entirely different bar down here. The space is much more industrial and holds the smell of booze and cigars. There are pretty girls dressed similar to the lovely Alicia bustling about to take care of the men's needs. A large area of the room is corded off like a boxing ring, without the elevation of such. The bar is more utilitarian than the one upstairs. What floors me is the room is packed. There has to be at least fifty people in here enjoying the place. I glance at my watch and it's about six o'clock. I didn't hear one inkling of this from upstairs.

"Locker rooms are that way. No one will fuck with your stuff if you put it in locker three. I suggest you not wear anything you want to keep clean. Fight starts in five minutes." Miles motions to the double doors on the opposite side of the room and then turns to head for a seat near the ring.

I chug the last of my beer and hand it off to a pretty little blond who winks as she passes by. Then I head for the locker room. My mind is racing that this is what I stumbled onto when I took down that perp the other night. The captain's going to shit himself when he hears about this, and we raid this place. Underground fighting is illegal. Sure, I'm about to take part in said illegal activities, but these assholes are going down. I strut into the locker room like the king cock I know I am. Too bad all the other king cocks aren't impressed.

It's then I am thankful that Cleaver and Hatchett had been working on this case before me. At least three of these guys are Santas hanging on the wall in the war room at the precinct. I strut up to locker three and start putting my things in when the guy next to me snorts a laugh.

"Looks like Santorro found himself a pretty boy to replace Jimmy. You got a name, pretty boy?"

"Yah. I do." I smirk as I pull my shirt off and toss it into the locker. A few of the other guys laugh as I give him the asshole answer.

The guy next to me narrows his eyes and I can tell he wants to get aggressive, but he's cut short by the short-stack of a guy that comes barking in. "First up is Caruso and… the new guy, Thatcher."

I give a nod to the man that doesn't even come up to my waist and finish putting my things in the locker. A quick glance around the room tells me no shoes in the fight. It's going to be rough going as I was not expecting to box today and wore jeans. I can only hope these assholes aren't half as good as I am.

The concrete is cold against my feet as I make my way to the ring. Caruso doesn't look too bad for a match-up. He is tall and lean versus my bulkier build. I roll my shoulders and flex my fingers in anticipation of the fight. We don't even shake hands before the bell rings, so I do what any good fighter does. I throw a right hook.

# CHAPTER FIFTEEN
## *Five Gold Rings*

"Jesus, Wolfe. Tell me at least you got a few licks in."

"You Should see the other guy," I grin, then wince from the pain.

She dabs the open cut above my eye with alcohol, then gently blows on it. I give her a goofy grin at the gentle gesture.

"So, fighting, huh?"

"Apparently. Looked to be an underground boxing ring. Well, figuratively, and literally. As far as I could tell, just a bunch of blue-collar people looking to make a couple of bucks doing what people have been doing for generations. Definitely will be a gold star in our book when we bust it up."

"You think busting a bunch of small-time broke guys is a gold star?"

"Well, not the people actually fighting in the ring. The people backing them. You should have seen Miles. He dropped at least five large on me and walked away with fourteen-to-one odds winnings. You don't do that kind of payout unless there is money there."

"Right. Which is why we can't bust it up," she dabs my knuckle roughly.

Between the pain, not thinking straight, and her shooting down my idea, I get a little shitty with her. "What do you mean, it's not worth busting? They got people there. They got books. People are throwing money around. We could get all sorts of people on illegal shit."

She heaves a sigh and gently wraps my knuckles in gauze. "Sure, Wolfe. Then the money comes in and lawyers up. Words like illegal search and seizure get thrown around. Followed by fruit of the poisonous tree. Next thing you know, we're looking like chumps in the courtroom and they're walking away. That bar closes, and another one opens, even harder to find."

"Damn it, woman. Don't you know I hate it when you use logic?" I don't know if it's the liquor talking, or the pain. "You sure we can't bust their asses?"

She actually laughs. It's a soft laugh, but she's laughing at me. "I promise, Wolfe. We'll bust the hell out of them, when we can get the big fish. Which means, you're going to have to swim upstream, and learn to keep your hands up," she teases as she returns to my brow and secures the bandage that was peeling off. I wince at the sharp stab of pain over my eye, and shy away from her hand.

"Fine. Fine. I'll go to the gym."

"No."

"No? What do you mean, no?"

"You'll go to their gym. You go to Miles and get him to get you a coach. He wants to make more money, right?"

I sigh, as once again, her logic is sound.

"You need to be their golden goose. Only way to get to the

big dogs is to be the best damn show pony out there."

I have to laugh at her mixing all these images together and then I do something out of character for me. I don't get attached. Not after what happened to Gracey. I would have married that girl had her shit brother not murdered her over the fifty bucks in the till. I slide my hand along her neck until my fingers are laced in her hair and I pull her into a kiss. It's everything I imagined kissing Trouble would be. Her lips are soft and full against mine as she reciprocates.

"You know, Wolfe. We're supposed to be working," she chastises softly when I break the kiss, but doesn't move away.

"I am working," I grin. "Isn't a prize fighter supposed to get a prize?"

"I thought the five hundred bucks Miles gave you was the prize."

"That's just the gas money that brought me to you." I don't know what's wrong with me, but I want her right now. Like a parched man in the desert, I draw her in to drink another kiss.

She settles into my lap, bringing her arms up to rest on my shoulders as we kiss. Whatever this is between us, I'm digging it. She deepens the kiss and presses her perfect body against me, allowing me to feel those sweet curves. The pain doesn't matter anymore as I slide my hands down to cup her ass and grind against her. I want to hear her call my name again. With a grunt, I scoop her up and keep her firm against me as I take us into the bedroom of this safe house.

******

When I open my eyes, Elle's nestled against me, using my chest as a pillow. Her body is sanguine and flush still from our evening together as she lays draped over me. The sweet scent of her shampoo mixed with the telltale scent of sex is definitely something I could wake up to every morning. I trail my fingers down her spine, enjoying the warmth of our bodies nestled together. It's early still, probably close to five in the morning, if I had to guess.

"Come on, Trouble. You need to get up and go to work."

"Trouble?" she asks in a groggy voice.

I grimace as I realize I called her that out loud. "With a capital T."

"Rhymes with P," she giggles against my chest.

"And that stands for Pool. Awoo."

Then I think this girl is part cupid, as she chimes in with the cutest, "Awoo."

Our moment is short-lived as she then pulls herself out of the bed and stumbles into the bathroom, closing the door behind her. By the time she comes back out, I am already dressed. "So, what's our next move if I can't raid the place?"

"I thought we already discussed this. Go get a fucking trainer," she hesitates, "from Miles."

"Oh. Yah. Okay. I vaguely remember that now."

"Jesus, Wolfe. How drunk were you?"

"Not?" I reply.

"Uh-huh. Do you remember the blow job?"

I scrunch my face up and struggle as I realize I don't remember much after the fight. It makes me take stock in my person. I remember fighting and sending Caruso to the ground. Then Miles congratulating me in the locker room with another beer.

"Awe, shit," I growl.

"What?"

"Last thing I remember is getting handed a beer and going out to revel in the success of my first fight."

Silence lingers between us, and she softens in her jabs at my memory. "For the record, there wasn't one."

I laugh at her priorities. "Okay, then."

"I need to get a blood sample. Maybe we can see what they gave you."

"Eh, I think at this point it's probably burned out of my system. But we can try." I'm a little nervous when she ducks back into the bathroom, then comes back with a blood drawing kit.

"Why do you have a leech kit in the bathroom of your safe house?"

"Why wouldn't I have one?" her tone is incredulous. She settles on the bed next to me and aptly draws my blood. This puts me even more ill at ease, that she knows how to do this.

"Exhale, Wolfe. See what you learn when you become a fed."

"I can't decide if you scare me or turn me on right now."

"Heh," she snorts. "Both." After she is finished playing vampire, she secures the sample and slides it into her jacket pocket.

"Don't drink anything else they give you. I bet that's how they get you to gamble and party."

"Won't it look suspicious if I suddenly become a teetotaler?"

"True. But if you don't remember anything at all. What happens when you do something you can't live with?"

"I'll try to pay attention to my drinking habit."

"Hmph," is her response. What is it with women only

responding with a noise? How am I supposed to translate grunting? I don't get the chance to call her on it as she comes over and plants a quick kiss on my forehead and takes off.

I rub my hand over my face and realize that I forgot to bring up the engagement. I was about to get ready to go to work myself, when I remember, I don't have work to go to. I sigh and gather my things. My soul dies a little again at the shit brown sedan. I could forgive them the car, but why that shade of brown? "Well, time to hit the grindstone," as I head out to find myself a payphone.

A couple of hours later, I am standing in a nondescript run-down boxing gym with Miles, in a suit, looking like he owns the place, grinning from ear to ear at me. "I guess you liked the gig, huh?"

"Eh, well enough. Dues are low, pay is decent. But I definitely need to brush up on my technical skills." I offer a boyish grin, trying not to look too cocky.

"Heh. I like you, kid." Miles chuckles as he clamps a hand on my shoulder. "I'm glad you came back. Let me introduce you to Red." He guides me to the ring.

The first thing I notice is the bruiser bouncing from foot to foot. He is throwing jabs and missing his opponent. Then grunting in pain as his opponent gets a few licks in. Miles gives a whistle and the two stop. The big guy goes to sulk in his corner, but the other combatant turns, taking the head pad off. There stands the cutest little redhead. Freckles sprinkled across her cheek, and her dark hair braided into a crown on her head. She ducks between the ropes and hops down to trot over.

"Why the feck are you here?" She chirps at Miles with an Irish accent.

"Got some fresh meat for you to tenderize." He nods his head in my direction.

I give her the smolder, my go-to for meeting a pretty face.

Sure as shit, she looks me up and down with disdain. "You fishin' em out of the gutter now, are ya?"

"North Pole."

"Nope. Nuh-uh. You ken I don't want nothin' ta do with the Santas."

"Eh. This one's a charity case."

"Don't feckin' care."

"Don't feckin' matter," mocking her accent. "He's yours now. He wins, you get a part of the cut, as per your union contract."

"You know what I want." she narrows her eyes at Miles.

"You damn well know it's not my call, sweet cheeks."

I stand in silence, watching these two have two conversations, the one they are saying out loud and the one they aren't saying at all. I'll be damned. Trouble is right... again.

There are bigger fish in this sea.

# CHAPTER SIXTEEN
## *Dashing Through the Snow*

My first day of training is hell. That girl knows how to throw a punch. Here I thought I knew how to keep my guard up, but I definitely learned my lesson today. She has been running me ragged around this ring. I have landed maybe a dozen hits, even fewer could be called good. I have been here since the sun came up, not having much else to do and wanting to avoid Maman ambushing me again. Plus, it is a good idea to teach myself how to fight again. Not the rules-laden police fighting, but the kick your ass under the bleachers stuff I used in high school.

By the end of the day, I can barely lift my arms. We had only actually spent about an hour in the ring. The rest of the time, she just had me swinging away at the bags, followed by running, lots of running. Then we were lifting weights, thankfully I am not so far out of shape that I cannot keep up. I glance at the clock, which is a mistake as she slaps my cheek.

"Pay attention, Princess!" She slaps my cheek again.

I can't help myself. I flash her one of my patented grins. "Just give it time, Red. We'll see who's the princess."

She slaps me again. "Focus!"

From the other side of the gym there is laughter and hooting, "Awe, Princess. You're not her type. Gotta be a real man to hook Red."

"Good to know, you're out of the running then," I clap back while focusing at the task before me.

"Oh. Princess got a mouth on her," one of the other shouts.

I laugh and shake my head, finish the reps.

"Good, now hit the showers, you stink. Be back at 5 a.m."

I manage to keep the groan at the idea of returning so early internal. But I do catch out of the corner of my eye, that every man is watching her walk to the showers.

This is too damn early for anything. I come walking in, on time, and she's bouncy, perky, and I think she has already had a full workout by the sweat on her brow. "Jesus, Red. Don't you ever sleep?"

"I'll sleep when I'm dead, Princess. Now it's time to run." She winks at me.

I drop my bag in the locker and follow, allowing her to remain a few feet in front of me the entire run. She really does have a great ass. About halfway through our run, she glances over her shoulder with a coy smile, then takes off like a rocket. "Keep up, Princess!" She calls back.

"Fuck," I mutter. Now I have to work at it. I can't let her win, or I will never get out of princess status. She's already preparing for a round in the ring when I come huffing and puffing through the door.

"Careful there, Princess, you might blow the house down."

"I... I'll... Live," I take a moment to hold my side as I gasp for air.

She beans me with a bottle of water. "You have two minutes to glove up and get in the ring."

"Sadist," I mutter.

"And proud of it! You wanted to be the best, right? Well, I'm the best. And knowin' Miles, you Santas fight every weekend. Which means I don't have enough time to train you proper, so you're gettin' the feckin' fast method."

"Good to know," I gasp out between gulps of water. I quickly throw my gloves on and haul my already sore body into the ring.

"So... How does a girl like you know a man like Miles?" I figure, if she's going to beat me down, I might as well get intel.

"Tell you what, Princess, you ring my bell and I'll tell ya." She winks at me.

"Challenge accepted," I smirk.

We throw punches and God help me; I keep my arms up today. I know, hitting a girl is probably not the best way to win her over, but Red isn't a woman. She's a fiery-haired demon with a nice ass and a great rack. Her fist connects with my jaw, and I hit the mat with a grunt.

"You know, Princess, you'd be better at fighting if you weren't thinkin' with your dick."

"Oh, well. Now that I know you're thinking about my dick, let's get this party started."

She blushes and my comment definitely throws her off just enough to get in for a good clean hit. Her head rocks back and she staggers a few steps to keep from falling over.

"Feck! That was dirty pool, Princess."

"You didn't say I had to play fair. So, about the union." I grin at her, triumphant.

"Two out of three! No cheating with dick!"

"Aw! Tease! Fine! Put 'em up! Put 'em up!" making my best

Cowardly Lion impersonation.

She laughs. "What? You gonna roar at me now?"

I wriggle my brows and turn up the smolder to eleven, "Rawr," I coo to her.

To which, she throws a punch. At least I am expecting it and block. We resume our flirty dance of fists around the ring until finally someone else rings the bell.

"Okay lovebirds, break it up. Time for someone else to use the ring," the owner barks up at us. Just like that, the fiery Irish woman turns into the ice queen again, and before I realize what's happening, I find myself on my ass again. That is one mean upper cut she has.

"Good hit," I groan. "You're gonna have to show me that move."

"Hmph," she grunts at me.

Is this something they teach women when they are in school? How to make a single sound mean a million things. I shake my head and pick myself up off the mat to get back to training. The rest of the day follows the previous day's formula, including telling me to be back at the ass crack of dawn.

Now knowing what to expect at the ass crack of dawn, I make sure to pick up coffee en route. I even brought her a cup. She chuckles and takes her cup, hoarding it to her, giving me the image of a small dragon huffing over breakfast. "Alright, I guess I'll go easy on you while we finish these."

Her definition of easy and mine are nowhere near each other until we're a good two miles from the gym and she plops down on an empty bench at a bus stop. She has barely broken a sweat, and I'm dying as I plop down next to her. I don't say anything immediately, grateful for the moment to drink the coffee I managed to not spill all over myself during our little warm-up.

"First, ya can't be talkin' about anythin' important to ya in the gym. People are always listenin'."

"Good to know." My breathing is under control, but my heart is hammering in my chest. I really need to lay off the fritters.

"Second, why do ya want to know anythin' 'bout me?"

"Hmm. Saw the way you looked at a certain union rep when he saddled you with me. I have enough sisters to know that look means trouble. Your end, or his?"

She gives me a funny look when I mention my sisters. I realize I have fucked up, but I let it ride, seeing how she reacts. If I try to back-peddle now, it definitely would be game over.

"Seems I'm not the only one with a few secrets." She chuckles as she takes a sip. "Been in the union since I was twelve. How about you? Money troubles?"

"Have you seen the car I drive? If you think my apartment's any better than that, whew." It's not a straight answer, but it's back on profile.

"Yah, I heard yer woman likes her champagne, too. Ya should be careful playin' with Miles an' his Santas. It's not all candy canes and cookies." She stands to continue the run and I grab her hand.

She turns back to look at my hand, then our gazes lock and I say in a quieter tone, "Seriously, if you need anything, just tell me." She definitely hit my 'big damn hero' button. There is no way in hell she is voluntarily part of this 'union'.

She snorts a laugh at me and yanks her hand free of my grip. "Feck off with your bullshit, Princess. Last one back to the gym, does 100 push-ups." Then she takes off running, at full speed.

I never should have given her caffeine. I enjoy the rest of my coffee before I even get up off this bench. I smirk, as she is long gone, finishing her lap. With a little stretch, I then turn and run back the way we came. Even with the extra mile, I know if I don't hotfoot it, she'll still be my ass there. I am huffing and puffing as I approach the door when she rounds the corner. The look on her face is priceless.

"Cheater!" She calls as she approaches.

"What? I beat you fair and square. You never said I had to follow you," I gasp out. "You said first one back."

"Hmph," is my only response. But, true to her word, she does a hundred push-ups. As punishment for being cheeky with her, I find myself also doing a hundred push-ups. I catch the faint smile on her face as we bob up and down on the floor.

# CHAPTER SEVENTEEN
## *Checking It Twice*

Elle left the safe house Monday morning with the vials of Joe's blood. She could see the worried look on his face that she even knew how to do this, which makes her grin. Having a Wolfe a little scared of her wasn't such a bad thing. Their night together had been hot as hell. That man knows his way around a woman, even if he was high as a kite. She drums her fingers on the steering wheel as she races to the federal building she works out of. Part of her hopes she can get this to the lab before her boss gets in and reams her a new asshole for recruiting Wolfe, after he told her to use a fed.

She trots up the steps, then laughs as she realizes she is humming a Christmas carol to the beat of her heels' staccato. "Fucking, Wolfe," she mutters and shakes her head. "Mornin', Earl!" She waves to the security guard at the front desk.

"Mornin', Agent Harris. Don't know what the hell you've done. But I'll give you five minutes to get coffee before I tell him you're in the building." His bass chuckles across the foyer.

"You're the best," she keeps the smile on her face until she's beyond the checkpoint and then she makes a b-Line for the lab.

The door swishes open, and the man in a lab coat looks up from his microscope. "No. Nuh-uh. Not happening."

"Even if it's a case of a cop bein' roofied?" She dangles the bag with the vials in it.

"You already got me in trouble for the profile. Why in the fuck would I help you further?"

"Because I'm your favorite? And I bring you the cool stuff? Did I mention it was a boy cop?"

"Okay. Now I'm intrigued," he takes the bag of vials. "How fresh is this sample?"

"Uh... Thirty or forty minutes old?"

"And when were they roofied?"

"Sometime yesterday."

"You're killing me, Harris. You know the chances are slim, at best, for this to come up with anything useful. Hair would have been better."

"I was a little pre-occupied."

"But not pre-occupied enough to get me a blood sample?" He eyes her dubiously.

She gives him an innocent smile. "I'll buy you a steak dinner," she tempts.

"Just get out of here before Frank catches us together. I'm already on thin ice."

"You're the best!" She leans over and kisses him on the check.

"Uh-huh. Now you're harassing me! Go on, get!"

Frank intercepts Elle in the first floor break room, where she is getting coffee. "Harris," he roars.

"Yes, sir?" She chirps as she pours him a cup of black coffee while filling her cream and sugar with a splash of coffee.

"Don't yes sir me. You damn well know what you did."

"Uhm… Booked the Santa assault kid?"

"Don't play coy with me, woman. I gave you a direct order and I find out from Hanson you still gave that ID to Wolfe. You lookin' to get fired, Harris?" He crosses his arms.

"Hanson's just sore I didn't pick him. Besides, Wolfe has the 'in' already. They approached him. Sending a fed in his place would have been game over and you know it." She offers him the coffee.

Frank narrows his eyes at the young agent. He hates when the rookies are right. But she needed to know he is the alpha here. He uncrosses his arms as he takes the coffee. Then sips the black bean juice of life while letting her stew under his intense gaze. He is sure she's fucking the boy, and this case is already compromised, but he'll pin it on her if there is any blow back. Half the boys already are gunning for her, and while he's hard on her, he knows she's a damn good agent. He couldn't suspend her right now based on the evidence she and Joe got. It would take too long to get another person up to speed and in good with Wolfe. "You know this cowboy shit don't fly. You've been lucky so far. Keep it tight and keep me in the loop, or I'll have your badge and your ass hanging on a wall."

"Yes, sir," she replies.

Tuesday Elle goes on the warrant scavenger hunt. She is armed with the information she did manage to get from Wolfe and knocks on every federal judge's door she can get to. By lunch time, she has heard everything from, "You got a nice ass, but I'm not giving you a warrant," to, "Get the fuck out of my office." Exasperated, she is sitting on a bench outside of her latest rejection's chambers. Glancing at the clock, she is contemplating what she wants to do for lunch when the cutest junior prosecutor plops down next to her.

"Rough day?" He smiles as he dangles a cup of coffee in front of her.

Elle's gaze pulls from the clock to the fresh-faced, pretty boy in a suit. She takes the coffee and suppresses the grimace at the bitterness of the untreated coffee. At least the boy prosecutor is pretty to look at. He did bring her a cup of coffee. She cracks a grin, "It's lookin' up," as she is unabashedly checking him out.

"I hear tell you're fishing for a warrant," he grins right back.

"Something like that. Got a solid case, just can't get a judge to sign off."

"Care if I take a glance?"

She eyes him and fishes out the request to offer it to him. When he reaches out to take it, she tilts away. "You're not fuckin' with me, are you?"

"Just here to give you an educated opinion," his smile is boyish with dimples, and is ever present.

She hands the file over and sips the coffee again while he reads it.

"No wonder you're not getting a judge to bite. You don't even know which bank you're wanting to pull records from."

"Well, it's not like I can just waltz in and ask the bartender for a statement."

"You know how bank managers could be. You find the right bank and I might be able to find the right judge." He winks at her and hands her file back.

Wednesday and Thursday are spent stalking the massive bartender when he closes up for the night, just hoping he goes to make the nightly deposit. Luck would have it, that Thursday night is deposit night.

Friday morning, she's leaning against the prosecutor's desk, actually wearing a skirt, and dangling her own cup of coffee in offering. He gives a low whistle when he walks into his office. "You even brought me coffee. You're my new favorite agent." He takes the coffee, sets down his briefcase and takes a seat at his desk.

Elle leans over the desk, knowing her blouse is unbuttoned one too many, proffers the amended warrant to him. "I believe you offered to help a young lady help find a judge?"

"I know just the judge for you. Follow me."

It's like magic. They are in and out in five minutes, and not one sexist remark made. Elle's beginning to think she wasted this perfectly good outfit.

"So, need any help picking up whatever you're gonna pick up?"

"Don't you have lawyer work to do?"

"Helpin' a federal agent serve a warrant is perfectly good warrant work."

An hour later, they are standing before a portly man at the bank. He looks the warrant over and sighs. He calls in his rather young secretary and sets her to work in making the copies of all the requested accounts. "And remember, sir. There is a gag order on this warrant. I'd hate to have to prosecute such an upstanding citizen for obstructing justice."

Elle laughs as the portly bank manager begins to sweat and nods anxiously at them. She casually picks up a business card for future reference. The manager looks from her to the prosecutor and tries to look casual as he sits back down at his computer and pecks at the keys. It takes several hours to photocopy all the items requested in the warrant. When the girl rolls out three boxes and scurries back into the copy room, Elle uses the phone to request a van. "Hope you didn't have any other plans today, champ." She chuckles at the prosecutor who rode in her car.

"Oh, I think me being here was my plan, right?"

She chuckles. "Slow day at the office?"

"More like I get to spend the day with one of America's finest agents."

Elle rolls her eyes and laughs.

Finally, the girl brings them eight boxes of paperwork in total. Elle watches the federal couriers load all of them and tag them appropriately for the chain of evidence before she signs off on the van driving them back to the office. "So, want me to drop you back at the courthouse?"

"Meh. I've been with you this long. Might as well help you sift through some of those numbers."

"You want to spend your Friday night sifting through the bank transactions of a run-down bar?" Elle raises a brow in suspicion.

"All depends on who you are sifting through bank notes with." He smiles as he gets into the passenger seat of her car.

"Suit yourself. Just remember when we miss dinner and you're eyeballs in boring ledgers." She slides into the driver's seat.

"I think I can risk it. Gives me a chance to see you in action."

# CHAPTER EIGHTEEN
## *O Holy Night*

Box after box, hour after hour, Elle and the dashing young prosecutor pour over bank statements, receipts, letters, and anything else related to the Wooden Nickel. The piles of papers have been stacked based on who they belong to. The sun has long gone down, and the Chinese food containers sit cold on the cabinet across the room. The two of them have been buzzing around each other in silence as they read document after document.

"Gideon," he chuckles as he leans back, threading his fingers behind his head.

"Come again?" Elle asks without looking up.

"My name, Agent Harris," he laughs then, "thought you might want to know it."

"Why is that?" She smirks, still not looking up.

"So, you know what to call out," he grins at her.

That gets her to stop and look at him. Her brow raises and her smirk turns into a feral grin. "That so? What makes you think I'm a screamer?"

"You strike me as the kind of girl that likes to tell the world just how much you like it."

Elle leans back, mimics his position, and looks him over. "You're pretty. I'll give you that. But it takes more than a pretty face to make me scream your name."

"How about witty banter, connections with judges, and a healthy bank account?"

"A federal prosecutor with money? Now I know you're lying. That's alright though. I don't need your money."

"That so? Cause you make so much working here?"

She snorts and gets up, coming around the table. "Tell ya what, Gideon, you make me scream your name, and I'll let you have a second date."

He leans up, bringing his face to inches from hers, and he smirks. "So, you do consider this a date?"

Her laugh is soft as she leans in closer, threatening to press her lips to his as she murmurs, "You did buy me dinner," she flicks her head toward the takeout boxes. "So, what do you say, champ? Think you're up for the challenge?"

He eases up from the chair, his hand sliding up her thigh until it rests on her waist. He stands at his full height, which forces her to tilt her gaze up. A step forward forces her to step back, but his hand holds firm on her waist, holding them impossibly close. Another step, then another, until their tango has her pinned against the wall and his lips press to hers, demanding she kiss him in return. "Challenge accepted," biting her lower lip.

His hands sliding down just enough to slip below the skirt. He follows the stockings up until he feels the panties against her soft skin. With a firm tug, he pulls them down to her knees, letting them fall the rest of the way to the floor where she delicately steps out of them. He enjoys the show, then he repeats it, so her skirt pools as well. His fingers splay over her skin, and he finds the sensitive spot nestled in her soft folds. He presses and rubs against her until her hips rock to meet him. His eyes never leave hers. He changes position with his hand, using his thumb to keep pressure on her clit as he slides his fingers into her. His other hand works his belt buckle, and he pulls his belt with one hand right from his waist. "What's my name?" he growls against her lips

"Mhmm," she hums in their kiss, getting a devious smile without saying any actual words. As she suspected, he rubs slower and firmer against her clit, teasing. She thought he might spank her with the belt in his hand, especially when he stops working her over to gather up her wrists. She allows him to bring them behind her back, then use the belt to bind them. "You're going to have to try harder than that, counselor," she coos.

He chuckles and trails kisses along her jaw to bite against her neck. "We're just getting started, Agent Harris."

He gently leans her back against the wall and begins unbuttoning her blouse she already had halfway undone to entice him. She has been teasing him all day, and he is going to enjoy this. His kisses move down and unclasps the front of her bra, freeing her perky breasts from the contraption. He draws a nipple between his teeth as he fondles the other breast.

Elle squirms and lifts to his kisses as he trails his fingers down to find her wet and wanting. He resumes the slow torture of her clit as he works his fingers in and out of her. "Say my name," he coos to her. She bites her lip harder and gives him a soft moan. He chuckles as he nips her breast again before moving to the other and rewarding it with a little tug between his teeth. His eyes sparkle with mischief. This girl is hot as hell, and quite comfortable being naked with him. It makes him hard just thinking about laying her out on the table. But a challenge is a challenge. She will call his name before he puts his dick in her.

Then he hears the belt hit the floor, and he grins as her fingers run through his hair, pushing his head down. "So demanding," he bites against her stomach, eliciting a chuckle from Elle. His fingers expertly work her, and her hips are rocking with him when his tongue flicks over her clit.

"Oh," she lets escape, and he knows he has her.

His fingers and thumb keep rubbing and teasing, as he watches her give herself to him eagerly. He is grinning as he lifts off her feet and turns with her in his arms, splaying her out on the end of the table they haven't covered in stacks of paper. His mouth is hot and biting as he nips at her breasts again. "What's my name?"

Elle casually drapes her knee over his shoulder and brushes her fingers along his cheek. "Oh, counselor, you're cute. But I'm not screaming anything without at least getting off once."

He smirks and then he leans down, burying his face between her thighs and his teeth rake over her clit as he sucks. "Oh, fuck," Elle gasps and lifts to him. His humming laughter against her is driving her wild. He expertly sucks against her while his fingers resume plunging in and out of her. His pretty blue eyes are watching her from his vantage point between her legs. How her hands naturally find themselves above her head, and how she arches like a bow pulled taught. It gives him the sexy view of her now crumpled dress shirt parted and open bra exposing those perfect breasts. But what really gets him going are the stockings without garters, the sheer black fabric shimmering in the office light, and those heels. He could watch her like this forever.

His tongue flicks along her throbbing clit he leans up and his grin turns feral when she moans and clenches on his fingers. Followed by the uncontrolled way her body milks his fingers, begging for him without a word from her sweet mouth. He watches as Elle's breathing is labored and how she looks like a cat who ate the canary. "Awe, too bad. Next time, counselor," she purrs.

"You tapping out, pussycat?" He stands then, unfastening his pants and sliding them down along with his boxer briefs. He couldn't wait any longer and wants her while she's too lost in her orgasm to leave him aching. Before Elle can make a move, he lines her up, letting her feel the swollen tip against her. Then he thrusts into her fully. His hands move to grope her breasts as he pumps hard into her. She brings her knees up and wraps her legs around him, locking her ankles at the small of his back. Which makes him grunt in effort as he leans over her more. His hands continue up and one rests on her throat, gripping just enough to let her know he is in control, and to keep her pinned to the table. "What's my name?" he slows to a teasing grind, letting her feel all of him press deep into her, only to retreat as far as her grasp on him would allow.

She grins and shakes her head as she bites her lip, but it soon gives way to a moan. She rocks her hips up to draw him in further.

"Nuh uh, only good girls get what they want," he teases.

"I am always a good girl," she breathes out.

"You, my dear," as he continues the slow pace, "are anything but a good girl."

"Stop talking and fuck me, Gideon," she hisses at him.

He smirks and resumes pumping hard and fast into her. His cock throbs with wanting release but he wills himself to wait. His only goal is to make her scream his name. As soon as she releases her ankles, he pulls out, making her yelp. He flips her onto her stomach, then presses right back to that shapely ass of hers, thrusting back in. He keeps her bent over the table as he pounds into her. He is grunting from the effort and his fingers press into the soft flesh of her ass to give him a better grip. When she goes to lean up, he slaps her ass hard, then pushes her back down.

Her moans are louder now as she pushes back against him. He's so close he can see stars behind his eyelids. Then he feels it, how her body tenses on him, milking his cock as he pounds into her. He has forgotten all about making her scream his name, but the moans coming from her are egging him on.

"Don't... stop...Fuck," Elle cries out.

Then he stops abruptly, buried deep inside of her. He holds stock still and keeps her pressed down to the desk with one hand.

"Gideon," she whines loud enough it echoes in the room as she tries to get him to finish her. As soon as the word leaves her lips, he resumes thrusting in her until he feels her body milking his hard cock. Her body jerks, and her moan is guttural like a sweet melody in his ears as she climaxes again.

"Good girl," he coos. "Now, turn around here and get your reward." He pulls her back, and then out of her, guiding her around and pushing her to her knees.

Elle is confused at first, lost in her orgasm, until she feels her knees buckle under her and he helps her to the right position, his tip brushing her lips. The taste of herself on him is as hot to her as him fucking her bent over the desk. Her lips part and she draws his head into her mouth, sucking hard.

"Fuck," he groans and pumps forward, lacing his fingers into her hair to tilt her head for him. Thrusting until he feels the back of her throat, then retreating. When her fingers curl around the base of his shaft and she swirls her tongue around the head, he loses himself. The explosion in her mouth makes her swallow hard and suck against his head to draw out the remains of his seed. When she finally releases his manhood from her lips, she reaches down and eases his clothes back up, fastening his pants before she reaches around and pats his ass.

"Good boy," she coos as she staggers back to her feet to find her skirt.

# CHAPTER NINETEEN
## *How The Wolfe Stole Christmas*

*December 13*

I stepped in the Wooden Nickel, expecting the place to be quiet, like it always is. I see six guys sitting around, enjoying beer. Bartender gives me a nod and motions me on in. None of these guys give me a second glance, though I feel like something's off. I descend the steps and the hallway is also full of people lined to one side. There are more people here than I thought would fit.

"Hey, kid!" Miles pulls me from the line, which makes me no friends, and walks me right to the front. "You got the entry fee for tonight?"

"Nah, man. Spot me? Paid all my bills and my girl took the rest." I lie. That money is being processed for fingerprints, though getting prints off of money is a long shot.

"I got you, kid. Go on in and get ready." He turns to the lovely young woman taking the entry fees and bets.

I almost felt bad, lying to them. I need them to believe I'm not someone smarter with money than most of these poor schmucks fighting. As I step through the doors, I am again surprised at the amount of people present. Men and Women fill every inch of what the regulars call the Pit. I finally make my way across to the massive chalkboard on the wall. There's my name, Thatcher, scrawled in the bookie's writing. The odds next to it are thirty-two to one for me to lose. Talk about killing my ego. I thought I had put up a pretty decent performance last weekend.

"It's not about you, Princess. They pulled in a ringer from the big leagues. Someone's gunnin' for ya."

I cast a glance at Red, who is probably the only woman in here not in a dress, and she has her arms crossed as she looks at the board, a frown on her face.

"That so? What for?"

"It's how they hook ya. Let me guess, you let Miles pay yer way in tonight, 'cause ya didn't have it? You feckin' yanks are so easy ta pull one on. It's a wonder you ever won yer freedom from the Brits."

I laugh, but I cut her a side glance. I figured this was how they got people wrapped up in this, what surprises me is she fell for this racket. "How much you in for?"

"None o' yer feckin' business, Princess. Yer business is ta win."

"If I win, do I get a reward?" I wriggle my brows at her, and she rolls her eyes half-heartedly slapping my face away.

"Get yer ass ready and don't be losin' tonight. Or yer gonna wish ya died when we start trainin' again."

I laugh and hold my hands up, backing away and then turning head into the locker room.

I am grinning as I walk in, ready for the smack talk I had last weekend. Only there is no one in here. I take a step back to make sure I didn't walk right into the women's restroom, not that there is one in this place. Then I step back in and head to my locker. Maybe the other guys are stuck in line.

I hear rustling coming from one of the stalls, and a grunt as the hidden person flushes. I think back to that damn chalkboard and realize there were only two names on it.

"Well, shit," I grumble. I rub my hand over my face and look to the ceiling as if I'm talking to God. "At least I'm the marquee fight. Yay?"

"You're in my way," a graveled and thick voice booms at me.

I glance over my shoulder to see who is starting shit already and what I see are peck muscles attached to the most impressive chest I have ever seen on a man. Then my eyes flick to his biceps. They have to be the size of my head. Following those massive muscles up, his shoulders twitch like a bird on a wire, giving way to a cue ball head, freshly shaved. I'm pretty sure this guy has three necks. All he is missing are the longhorns and I can put his ass out to pasture to stud.

"My bad," as I then saunter over to my locker. His non-committal grunt tells me I am not about to be shoved into said locker. There is not a word between us for the next hour as we prepare to fight. I can hear the roar of the crowd outside of the locker room. Someone found a microphone. Or is it a megaphone? They do sound a fair bit like a Peanuts adult. I remove my boots, and shirt. The chicks dig the shirtless guy. To be fair, I don't think the other guy could fit in a shirt if he tried. Next thing I know, they're banging on the door, telling us it's time to head to the ring.

What have I gotten myself into this time?

I shove my way through the crowd to finally get into the ring. When I turn around, it's like watching Moses waving his holy staff to part the damn sea. Then the chanting starts. I am not sure what this guy's name is between, Thrasher, Thresher, and Crusher. It doesn't matter. Those are all bad options. Red was right, this fight is rigged. Whatever his name is, doesn't even try to hide it as he comes walking out with brass knuckles. This is going to suck.

My eyes scan the crowd and the first thing I see is Miles, grinning like an idiot. The second is a man dressed in a pin-stripe suit next to him, looking like the proverbial sore thumb amongst the sea of blue collar folk in their Sunday best. The third, is Red, suddenly looking quite blue around the gills. Our eyes meet and she mouths to me, "Keep yer fecking hands up," motioning with her hands to block.

It is not going to matter what I put in front of one of those bulldozers, if that bull connects, he's breaking something of mine. It's a good thing we have been working on building my stamina, because this is about to be my best Jack-Be-Nimble impression, and he's one hell of a candlestick.

The portly schmuck that pretends to be ref steps between us. "Rules are, anything goes. First one knocked out loses." I tilt my gaze up to Mr. Bull and I see the fat fuck of a ref fling himself out of the path as that freight train plows full speed at me. I spin in time to watch his soccer ball sized fist whiz right in front of my face. I don't stay put. I keep spinning, as I feel his other fist glance off my shoulder. Pretty sure I just pulled off a flawless pirouette to avoid becoming ground Wolfe. My back is against his as he swings his left arm in a backswing that I am sure would decapitate me.

Thankfully, he overextends himself and one donkey kick later, he is on his knee. I think it's a great idea to follow my donkey kick with a roundhouse knee to his temple, which connects, by the way. Then I am laying on my back, the wind knocked out of me as he throws me like a fucking sack of potatoes to the ground. I would have thought a knee to his temple would have done something useful. I don't have long to reflect on this matter as I am forced to roll away from the incoming wrecking balls he calls fists, causing them to pound into the concrete next to me.

"GET OFF YER FECKING ARSE!" I hear the high-pitched shriek of Red over the crowd.

"Workin' on it," I mutter as I finally get breathing room between us. I can see I have done some damage. I watch him favor his left leg as he pushes himself back to his feet. I bounce from foot to foot, with one fist down and one fist up, waiting to see my opening. Unfortunately for me, this is no longer a quick and easy win for him, as we Wolfes are wily. We are here to entertain the masses, after all.

I watch him stagger forward and I dance around him like a two-bit stripper to a pole. The crowd is closing in on us, to cut off my escape routes, which allows him to land a few glancing blows. Even with blocking, it still feels like a sack of bricks slamming into my body every time he connects.

His face is red, and veins are bulging as we both are covered in a sheen of sweat. I'm pretty sure they killed the AC to rile everyone up. The roar of the room is deafening. All I can see is the murder in his eyes. If he gets a hold of me, I'm dead. I happen to enjoy my life right now, thank you very much.

So, what do I do? I egg this motherfucker right on by planting my feet and making kissy noises at him. It's like the matador waving the red cape before the bull. I can see his vision turning red with fury from me taunting him. The crowd whistles and cheers at the showmanship.

"What the feck are ya doing, Thatcher?" Red screams.

Then he charges forward, closing the few feet I had put between us. Sensei Kreese's immortal wisdom fills my head, and I smirk. I dance to the side in the most perfect slide to the left, avoiding his meaty paw. Then I plant my right foot to kick down and forward with my left, trying not to wince as the sickening sound of Mr. Bull's knee shatters and his leg bends the wrong way.

I don't have time to enjoy my victory blow, as that brute thrashes in place like a windmill of death. I take a few clipping blows as I finally get in behind him. I leap on him like a teenage girl in a fight over a boy at school. My knees latch onto his ribs and my arms around at least two of those three necks as I pull my wrist back, squeezing as hard as I can.

I almost lose my grip as he bucks like the steer he is and slams me into the concrete under him. I grunt in pain, but I'm not letting go. I already caught this bull by the horns. Eight seconds later he finally stops bucking and his hands go lax. I hold on for another second or two, to make sure he's not playing opossum. Then I realize, I have to get out from under this asshole. This is the second motherfucker I have had to get out from under in as many weeks. At least that Santa only weighed about a buck fifty. This guy has to be at least three hundred pounds. I grunt and groan, wriggling and writhing until I get to my feet.

The room is deadly quiet. Not even a peep from Red as everyone watches the portly ref kneel and check for a pulse. I hold my breath, namely because I'm pretty sure my ribs are cracked. The idea of killing a man for sport is making me sick to my stomach. It feels like an eternity the seconds it takes for him to check my opponent for a pulse.

"He lives! Thatcher wins!" The ref shouts and scrambles back.

Like the sea closing in on Pharaoh's soldiers, the mass of onlookers bum rush me in congratulations. I don't know how I manage it, but I weasel my way out of the sea and back into the safety of the locker room. I'm not in here two minutes before Miles comes bursting through the door like a raging bull himself.

"What the fuck was that, Thatcher?!"

# CHAPTER TWENTY
## *Rejoice! Rejoice!*

"I think someone's pissed about charity cases," I joke, but I am confident my ribs are cracked. Maybe bruised, but definitely in pain. I don't turn to face Miles as he starts in his rant about how much money he has lost, that I owe him big, and this wasn't how it was supposed to be. I think the man's off his rocker, or drunk. Maybe they have slipped him a little of what they slipped me the last time I was here. I move by him and tug out several paper towels and turn on the cold water. I'm covered in sweat and blood, still floating on the high of kicking that bull's ass.

"Are you fucking listening to me?" Miles snarls as he jerks me around to face him.

Instinct kicks, and before I can catch myself, I throw a hard left jab into his stomach.

He lets out this donkey wail noise as all the air puffs out of his mouth. His eyes bulge and he doubles over.

"Shit! Sorry! I was... Hey man, deep breaths. Come on. You got this. Fuck, Miles. I'm sorry!"

The slow clap that echoes in the locker room pulls me from trying to help Miles work through being sucker punched to searching at the source of the clap. Near the door is the man I noticed before the fight. I stand up straight and square my shoulders. I don't know this guy from Adam, and well, I already rendered Miles useless. He'll think twice before putting hands on me after a fight. "What the fuck do you want, Daddy Warbucks?"

"Clean yourself up, kid. I'm not here to fight," he is laughing at the situation. "But I see you've taught Miles a valuable lesson."

I cut Miles a glance and shrug, turning back to the sink. I keep my head down as I work to clean myself, but I'm definitely watching the two of them, and listening.

"I think you need to cash out, Miles. The kid's mine. As I no longer have a fighter for next week."

"Wh-what? The fuck you are. The kid's my Santa."

The man in the suit clicks his tongue and shakes his head. "And you have the buy in? I believe you were just raving about how the kid lost you... three-hundred? Or was it four-hundred-thousand?"

I stiffen as it clicks into place what Miles has done. That asshole bet on me to lose the fight. I should punch him again. Daddy Warbucks sees the red in my eyes and grins a little.

"Get out of here, Miles. Or I will be forced to relay tonight's outcome to the union president."

I throw the used paper towels in the trash can, satisfied I have cleaned as much blood as I'm going to get off me, and saunter back to my locker. I'm still feeling like king cock, even if Miles tried to rig it against me. With a thump, I open my locker I pull my T-shirt over my head first, then snatch my socks and boots out. When I sit on the bench, Warbucks sits next to me. I ignore him. He has said nothing particularly useful, other than confirming that even he answers to someone else. Yeah, I caught that bit, and I'm ready to take this dog and pony show on the road, anyway. With a wince and a grunt, I pull on my socks and shoes.

"You have promise, Mr. Thatcher," his voice is calm, and he seems like he isn't put out that I boxed his fighter right into the hospital. Fuck me, the paperwork on that is going to be a bitch. I hope Trouble's got my back when the time comes to explain that.

"That so?"

"It is if you want to make ten times what you make here. This is just the stepping stone, Mr. Thatcher. Fighting for me is an opportunity. One that a person in such a financial situation as yours would be foolish to pass up."

We stare each other down, and finally I sigh. I can feel the adrenaline coming down and could use a beer and a juicy burger. Or Trouble. Hot damn, why not all three? Now I'm thinking of my partner and what she did to me in Mrs. Gayle's office while trying to look tough in front of the guy in the suit.

He thrusts his hand out and offers to shake, "Mr. Tomlin."

"Thatcher," as I take his hand to shake.

"I know all about you, Erik," Tomlin gives me a fatherly smile. "You should rest. Your next fight is Saturday. I will have your trainer fill you in on Monday." He stands and clamps a hand on my shoulder with a pat. "I do not take well to losing, Mr. Thatcher."

"So, I guess that means today was a pretty shitty day for you, huh?" I give him a smug look.

Mr. Tomlin's face spreads into a wide grin and he shrugs, neither confirming nor denying what kind of night he has had before he leaves the locker room.

Five minutes later, I'm walking out of the bar. It's empty other than a few drunks moping over beers at the bar proper.

"Thatcher, hold up," Alicia's sweet voice chirps from her perch behind the glass. I realize now that taking the money in doesn't get protected but paying out does. She motions with her head to the little door I hadn't noticed before in the niche. She disappears from the window and the little door swings open. It's dark in this cubby and she's keeping the door close to her.

I furrow my brow and am worried she is about to ask me for help. Glad I didn't drink anything tonight, as it looks like I'm destined to box. She thrusts a manila envelope the size of a red brick into my hand, and it has been taped with clear packing tape, at least twice. "What's this?" I drop my voice low.

"That's your winnings. Miles paid your way in, but he put it under your name, not his. Payouts only go to the name it's under. That's the rule."

"That's cause that asshole expected me to lose," I give her a wolfish grin.

She frowns. "You watch yourself, Thatcher. These men don't like to lose, and you cost a lot of people a lot of money tonight."

My grin fades pretty damn quick. "How much?"

She gives me a pointed look and closes the door in my face.

I exhale dramatically and roll my shoulders as I tuck my winnings into my jacket, zipping the inner pocket closed. I rub my hand over my face, and I trudge back up the stairs, ready to face my doom.

Oddly, I make it up and out of the Wooden Nickel without

any altercation, and when I come barreling through the door, there is not an angry mob like Alicia suggested there would be. What I do find, much to my delight, is a hot little red-head leaning against that shit-brown box they call a car. I'm imagining her on the hood of my Firebird as I stalk toward her, my wolfish grin re-appearing.

"Took ya long enough. Were you and Tomlin fecking in the locker room?"

I stop just in front of her, kind of caging her in. From here I can smell the whiskey on her. "Looks like I'm movin' into the big leagues. I believe you owe me a reward." I tease her about our last conversation at training, where she said if I won tonight, she would give me a reward. Her laugh is soft, not her usual guffaw at my misfortune. There is a mix of emotions I can't read on her. She eases off that car and presses right to me.

"Take me home, Thatcher," her voice is sultry, and I am instantly hard.

"Yes, ma'am," I drawl as I open the passenger door for her.

It's not a long drive to her place. I guessed right in that she is within walking distance of the gym. We don't say a word, heading into her apartment. I keep my eyes on her the entire time, but I quickly realize she has no intention of sticking around. The two duffel bags by the door are packed to the gills. I don't say anything. I pull her into a heated kiss. Her lips are soft and sweet from the whiskey. She wins a groan of pleasure from me when her hands brush against my still hard dick through my pants. It does not take me long to realize she's fumbling. That's alright, she's drunk.

I deepen the kiss and plant my hands on her hips to walk her back to the little bed I see shoved against the floor to ceiling window. My kisses trail down along her neck and the sweet little noises she makes tells me she likes it. Again, we work on getting our clothes off. I have her down to nothing but her panties in no time flat. I'm less undressed and I give her a light ass slap before I toss her down on the bed and finish the job for her. I swear to God, I'm the luckiest bastard around. She's hot as hell with that pale skin and red hair. Little freckles kiss along her skin as I drop to my knee, and I part her legs to admire my little boxing demon.

She blushes, and it only makes her more beautiful. I kiss my way up along her thigh, then to her stomach, nipping her skin as my hands reach down between us and I begin to stroke my fingers along her panties, applying just enough pressure to reward me with sweet little moans. Her body arches under me and I lean up, watching her writhe on my probing fingers as I slip them under the panties. This girl's tight as hell on my fingers and I didn't think I could get harder, but here we are. I rock my fingers faster, smirking at how wet this makes her. I don't say a word, while I'm admiring her. I know that Red's got a smart mouth, and one wrong word will end this vision in front of me.

It's painful not claiming her like I want to. There is something nagging me about this, though. I want it. I can feel the raging hard-on spurring me on. Maybe it's the cop in me, maybe it's the disapproving look of Elle that flashes in my mind, but I hesitate. I rub her clit with my thumb as I shift my hand around.

"Thatcher," she whines the only name she knows for me, and I frown. My hard-on fades and I realize why I can't follow through. She's not into me. She's into Thatcher, a thug she boxes with. Tomorrow, I would be the bad guy and the last thing I want is to complicate this by having sex with her. I'm thankful her eyes are closed, and I lean down over her, kissing against the hollow of her neck, up along her jaw, until I pull her into a heated kiss. I grin as she moans against my lips, and I feel her body clench on my fingers. Her nails dig into my arm, and I pump my fingers into her while rubbing her clit until I feel the last shudder of her orgasm.

I lay propped on my arm alongside her. Her eyes flutter open, then closed again, and she smiles. A bit of snuggling and a few content sighs escape her before I realize she is fully asleep against me. I remove my hand from between her legs and ease out of the bed to duck into her bathroom. I turn the water on and look at myself in the tiny mirror. I couldn't help but think there was something off about this. It was too damn familiar to let it go. I stare down at the running water and that's when it hits me. "Fuck," I shut off the water and stalk back into the room, getting dressed.

I lean over her and pat her cheeks, "Come on, baby girl. I need you to wake up." She is breathing slow and steady. Her cheeks are flushed, and she doesn't respond. I check her pulse and it's strong. I pat her cheek rougher, and she still does not respond.

"Damn it. I hate it when I'm right." Sure, it could just be the booze and my stellar performance, but somehow that doesn't add up.

I quickly find pajama shorts and a T-Shirt to pull on her. Then I scoop her right up. She is lighter than I expected, which I am thankful for as every step sends searing pain through my rib cage. A quick drive to the hospital and I get her into the emergency where my theatrical performance as Thatcher creates enough chaos for them to take her and for me to slip away.

I hit up the payphone outside the emergency room doors to let Agent Harris know about Red when a man answers her phone.

# CHAPTER TWENTY-ONE

## *All I Want for Christmas*

I stop when I hear the man's voice. I'm not sure if it's the situation with Red, the afterglow of the fight, or that this motherfucker is in Elle's place in the middle of the night, answering her phone like he lives there, but I'm suddenly raging bull pissed. Fuck, I hope he doesn't live there. Wait, I know he doesn't live there. I've stayed the night. Wait, why the fuck is he staying the night? I run my fingers through my hair as I realize I am angry that he answered the phone. It's taking all my willpower to not just drive over there and show him who the fuck gets to stay the night.

"Hello," I hear the man say again and I hear Trouble in the background asking who it is.

"Put Elle on," I growl at him, forgetting all my manners. I listen to the shuffling noise and shift my weight around, trying to think rationally.

"Hello?" Elle's sleepy voice comes across the phone.

"Who was that?" I bark like a jealous boyfriend. I rub my hand over my face and know I need to calm down. She's not my girl, even though she lied to her whole family, telling them we are engaged.

"None of your fucking business, what do you want?" Her voice was no longer that sultry sleepy sound and holding a menacing promise of tearing me a new asshole.

"What I want is for you to get your ass down to County General. There's a cute little redhead that needs Mamma Elle to nurse her wounds. Seems she has trouble holding her liquor, too." Jesus, I hate this spy talk. All my anger vanishes with the efforts I have to put in to alert her to Red having been roofied, without actually letting the other person I know is there know anything. Not that I think she is letting him listen, but better safe than sorry. I pray she picks up what I put down.

There is a silence in response. I worry she is just going to hang up on me, and not do anything about it. Damn feds, always leaving the rest of us high and dry.

"Thanks, I'll take care of it," then she hangs up on me.

I sigh in relief as I hang up the phone. I'm frustrated and angry. Red can't be much older than Carrie was. Just the thought of Carrie's name makes my chest tight. I still have the ring I was going to give her. She was the one, the shining light in this fucked up world. I went to that diner nearly every damn day just to see her pretty smile and listen to her sass all the cops. I shove my hands into my pockets as I stalk toward my car. She had never hurt anyone and her brother, of all the lowlifes out there, had stabbed her to death. The images of her covered in blood, and the shocked look on her face haunt me. I swore then I was never letting myself get that close to a woman.

I jerk open the car door and throw myself in. It's eating me alive that some asshole answered Elle's phone. Who is he? How long have they been seeing each other? Does she like him more than me? "Fuck," I growl out loud as Meg was right, I do like her. "No," I bark at myself. "Nuh-uh. She's a fed. She's your best friend's kid sister. Well, ex-best friend. But still. It's the principal of the matter." I need to get Elle out of my system. How did I let this happen?

By the time I get home, I'm in no mood to talk, but I see Meg standing there in her God damn thong and tank-top. I don't even bother to say hello. I step into the kitchen, and she turns to face me. The yelp she makes in surprise makes me smirk. I just lean down and throw her right onto my shoulder. I don't even care if it makes her drop the coffee mug that is in her hand.

"Joe," she giggles and whines at me.

"Shut it," I slap her ass, and I kid you not, this girl wriggles for more.

I stalk like the caveman I am to her room, and I throw her down on the bed. I tear out of my clothes like a man on fire. Then I drop onto my knees, pulling her legs apart. She's breathless and beautiful underneath me. Her cheeks are flush and she's giggling still at my lack of manners. I stop, watching her silently, the question in my eyes to see if she wants this. I want to bury myself in her and forget that I'm starting to have feelings for Elle. Feelings I don't want to have.

"Jesus, Joe," she gasps at the sight of me. I had forgotten that I am all banged up. Her expression tells me I am about to be cock-blocked twice tonight from this fight. I thought Rocky always got the girl, boy was I wrong.

I watch as her expression takes me in, and then she rolls off the bed. "Come on, let's get you cleaned up."

Okay, maybe this isn't such a bad plan. I perk back up and follow her into her bathroom. She faces me after turning the shower on and starts stripping herself. "As cute as you are, Joe. That," motioning to my banged up body, "does not make the go-go juices go."

I laugh at her choice of words, but I nod, stepping into the shower with her. It's not long before she's lathering me up and wiping away the night's festivities. Once I get go-go juice approved clean, she works her way down and I watch in fascination as she sucks my dick like I'm the best damn popsicle she has ever had. I kill the water and I enjoy her mouth. My only problem is I close my eyes while it's happening. It's not Meg that's on her knees then, it's Elle, with that smug look she had on her face in Mrs. Gayle's office. Fuck, why can't I get that woman off my mind?

Meg and I get dried off and head back into her room where I join her on the bed.

"No, you need to bandage that," she motions to my ribs.

"I'll be fine." Then I suck in air between my teeth when she touches the bruised spot.

"Uh-huh. This will help you with that problem," she brandishes the ace bandage and then settles behind me on the mattress. "So, you want to tell me what that welcome home was really all about?"

"No," I grumble as I hold my arms up for her to wrap.

"Carrie again?"

"How did you—. No!" I narrow my eyes at her. But the look she gives me tells me she could read me like an open book right now.

"So, then it's about Agent Harris."

"You sure you aren't a cop?" I flash her a grin.

"The only difference between a stripper and a cop is a badge."

"Wait. How do you figure that?"

"We both shake down men for something we want without actually touching them."

"I... don't shake down people."

"Uh-huh," she grins. "All you need in one of those interrogation rooms is a pole."

Now I'm grinning, thinking about the captain ranting about a pole in his bullpen.

"Don't change the subject. You wanted to fuck me until you forgot. What's up?"

I love Meg because she knows me. I rub my hand over my face. "There was a guy at her place."

She brings her damn hand up like it's a phone and then says, "Uh... Hello, Mr. Kettle. One moment, let me give you to Pot."

I roll my eyes and grumble. She isn't wrong. "I'm not the one that told everyone we were engaged," I mutter.

"But you went along with it. I heard what you didn't tell Mrs. Wolfe."

"That's different," I try to dig myself out of this.

"Nope. You like her," she teases me as she flops back on the bed, making her perfect tits bounce.

It's distracting, so I turn to face her door and rest my elbows on my knees. I stare at the door and then I feel her behind me again, rubbing my back in comfort. "Agent Harris isn't Carrie, Joe. It's okay to like her. But you can't be pissed about her sleeping with another guy when you haven't staked your claim. You know that's not how this works."

"It's only been six months." I feel guilt welling up, like I have tarnished the memory of Carrie somehow.

"So. You were fucking everything that walks trying to forget your feelings for Carrie. Now, you're not even into when I give you head in the shower. Nothing says you have to marry Agent Harris. But maybe you should stop bein' a dick about it and tell her how you feel." She pauses then and I can almost feel the laser focused look from behind me. "You didn't lose your shit with her, did you?"

"What? No. We're partners. I just... She was asleep. I think. He answered... and... Fuck," I groan and Meg laughs.

"Easy, tiger. It's alright. We all fall in love."

"I'm not in love, Meg. I'm..."

"Twitterpated. Look, Joe. There are two ways to handle it. One, you tell her you're into her and see what she says. Or two, you don't. And you quit being shitty when she hooks up with someone else. Now, get out, I have a double shift and need to sleep. And don't forget to clean up the mess you made in the kitchen."

I mutter something uncouth about kicking her ass to the curb as I leave the room, but we both know that's an idle threat.

## CHAPTER TWENTY-TWO
### *We Three Kings*

I spent all of Sunday relaxing. As much as I wanted to check in with Agent Harris every five minutes, I know that if we're caught together, I would blow my cover. Not to mention, I'm avoiding her like the plague. I don't want to deal with what Meg said last night and am thankful she had to leave for work while I was asleep.

Monday morning, I roll out of bed at four thirty, knowing I don't want to be late to the gym. At minimum, I want to have a little chat with Miles about betting against me. A quick shower and a cup of coffee later, I'm trudging into the gym.

"Thatcher!" The boys circle up, and I'm patted on the shoulder and revered. Guess I'm no longer a princess. I can't say I miss the nickname. Then I see Miles, he is leaning against a wall, his arms crossed. I saunter over and hold out my hand.

"No hard feelings, man." I keep my face neutral in spite of wanting to beat this prick into the wall.

He snorts and brushes my hand away as he stalks off.

"Ah, pay him no mind. He's still sore he lost a lot of money," one of the guys reminds me.

I have done nothing with my winnings. I know I should put them into evidence, but I have a better idea. What the feds don't know won't hurt 'em.

The guys fall into their workouts and I'm left looking around, so I tape up and I find a bag. At eight, I am about to call it for the day, when Tomlin and another man come walking in. I shift around the bag to get a better look at them without giving away I'm really watching them, and I listen.

"Any of you seen her?"

"Nah. She's in the wind. She really buy herself out?"

"She bet on the kid and won a lot of money. What do you think?"

"Still, you think she would run?"

"Well, she was not at her place when we came to check on her."

I freeze, mid-punch. Those fucks were coming to collect her. What would they have done had we been there? I roll my shoulders a little, trying to not look right at them. I toss my anger into hitting the bag. I can only hope Elle took care of the girl.

Then the two men make their way to me. "Thatcher, meet Gavin. He'll be training you for the fight next week."

"Where's Red?" I grouse. "She's my trainer."

A smirk forms on Tomlin's face and he shrugs. "It would seem she has vanished. She had taken a shine to you, from what I have been told."

I shrug and stop my punches to turn and shake hands with Gavin. I give him a once over for anything remarkable about him, but am greeted with nothing that could be useful. His grip is strong, and he smiles at me.

"This kid is the one to take him down? You're shittin' me,

Tomlin."

"I assure you, I am not shitting you. Erik Thatcher is an astonishingly good fighter. I trust you will make him ready for Saturday."

"Yes, sir."

Tomlin leaves and then I spend the rest of the day being put through the paces like a show pony. Gavin's a great boxer, but he's not Red. That girl can fight.

******

I make sure to pick a lull in the day at the hospital. I did not want to be seen or have to explain myself to very many people. I flash my badge at the cute little nurse, and she happily shows me where "the bull" is resting. With a smirk and a quick kiss on the cheek, she hurries back to her station. I look left and right to make sure there is no one paying attention and I ease open the door.

It's quiet inside, and the bull is sulking in his hospital bed, changing the channels on his television.

"What the fuck do you want?"

"Hey man, I feel bad... I mean... about the knee." I motion.

His eyes narrow at me, and I can see the debate going on in his eyes to determine if he can beat me down from his position. I wait for him to throw me out, or to question why I would come here.

"What's it to you?" His voice sounds like he's a mouth breather with a load of snot lodged in place.

I slip out the envelope, and I move to the chair with his jacket in it. I haven't even bothered to count how much it is. I know it's a lot, based on Red telling me what she had won. This only wins me another suspicious look and I shrug.

"Take it, or don't. Give it to charity for all I care. But get the fuck out. Don't know what they did with Red, but she's missing after paying Tomlin." I know it's a risk, but his expression is one of surprise and worry. It tells me more than any words would.

He thinks they have done something nefarious with the little demon. He grunts and nods, so I leave.

******

I spend the week training and harassing people about Red's whereabouts. On Wednesday, I noticed a car following me home. Meg greets me at the door with a heated kiss and I ease my arm around her, sliding back into the apartment. The guy she had been seeing was found with his pants around his ankles and one of the other girls bent over a chair. I'm happy to oblige her need to fuck him out of her system, but it makes me forget about the car following me.

Saturday finally rolls around, and I head to the address given by Gavin. He had instructed to dress nicely, but I didn't want to show I had money for a suit. So, I, against my upbringing, show up in khaki pants and a button down dress shirt.

If I thought the Wooden Nickel was a hidden gem, this place is a fucking invisible super jet. On the outside, it's a warehouse, rundown and broken, near the river. We cross the threshold, and it is dark for a good ten seconds while the outer door closes. I roll my shoulders, half expecting to get jumped.

"Relax, kid. No one's going to give a shit about you until you win. That hole Miles is running is small potatoes compared to this. He tried to get cute, and it cost him. Tomlin's not so ignorant."

I nod and blink as my eyes adjust to the lighting revealed by the inner doors opening. The inside of this place is swank. Velvet drapes, leather booths, dark-stained and polished tables set the stage. There are three bars, and several casino tables. There are men in suits, and women in barely any clothing. Unlike the Nickel, this place has nice music playing in the background, and there is not a concrete 'pit' for fighting. In fact, this room doesn't look like it will hold a fight.

"This way," Gavin motions and I follow.

We pass through another set of doors and into the fighting area. Down the arena steps and across the sand covered floor, I turn my head back once to see if anyone followed.

"Listen, kid. Don't get cocky. You're good. Damn good. But these men aren't desperate for cash and fighting to just survive. These are the made men. They are well paid, highly trained, and protected. The Santa gag is just to see who makes the grade for the Nickel. You took out the reigning champ in this circuit. Play your cards right and you'll live like a king."

I nod again, and he holds open a door for me.

"Your locker room. I'll be back in about thirty minutes. Don't talk to anyone and don't leave this room until I tell you to. Security here will bust your knee cap first and ask second."

"Got it," I say in a clipped tone. I am relieved to not share a locker room, but that makes it damn hard to overhear anything. I don't have time to protest as he turns on heel and leaves immediately. The silence is peaceful as I get ready for the fight. I'm still feeling all the injuries from last week, but I need to push through. Even if I lose tonight, I'm still moving up in this world.

It's at least an hour before Gavin returns. Then he leads me out to the ring. The arena theater is packed. The noise of so many people socializing in a closed space is amping me up. There are drinks clanking, and the heavy scent of cigars in the air. I smirk and my movement gains in swagger the closer to the ring we get.

"Remember, kid. Keep your hands up. This guy likes to cut up under the chin and make your teeth crack or cut your gums." I nod once and then we're moving to the center of the floor. The sand between my toes reminds me of a trip to the beach in France when I was little. The ref says something, but I'm not paying attention. I'm watching my opponent. The bell rings and everything else fades away.

# CHAPTER TWENTY-THREE

## *Christmas Bells Are Ringing*

We dance around the ring like two predators circling our prey. He makes the first move, tiring of my smirking face taunting him. Damn he is fast.

He jabs and I juke.

Blows are landing on both sides, and every time he hits my ribs, I swear I see stars. I have no business fighting tonight. I figured the racket out though. They lift you up just enough to suck you in further. I have no idea how much I'm out if tonight goes poorly.

I finally get a right hook in that sends him sprawling into the ropes. I don't give him a second to catch his breath as I sprint forward and come with a hard kidney punch that makes him bounce off said ropes.

He grunts and spits on the mat. He tried to twist out of my attack, but I see him stagger.

Another quick step and I throw a punch to his gut. It's a mistake and I have to give him props for setting up the trap. I leave myself completely open, thinking I could hit him hard enough to send him to the mat.

He curls in on himself, taking the blow to his arms and continuing his momentum forward until he is bent over. His leg comes up, planting his knee hard into my rib cage.

I let out a gasp of pain, and I can't breathe. It makes me stagger back, and he is on me.

His fists fly one after the other, right into my chest and gut. It is taking all my strength to not double over. Tears are in my eyes as I think I'm going to puke.

I don't care how dirty it is, I need this guy off me, and fast. So, I lean into the punches and rear back with my left fist, curling up and hard, right into his jewels.

There is an audible gasp and a squealing whine from him as the fists stop.

The roar of the crowd dulls, and I pull myself upright, allowing him to retreat. We're both bloody and in pain. I know he's pissed and how he looks at me says I won't be making any friends anytime soon. I would like to say I feel guilty, but that just isn't the case. I feel fucking great for being so clever. But I want this over, so I stalk forward, ignoring the pain blazing through my body.

He tries to flee but is limping. I must have got him clean in his junk. I'll apologize later. I get ahold of his shoulders, and give him another knee to his chest, throwing him to the mat.

Then the bell rings.

"Winner - Thatcher!"

Just like that, it's over. I watch as a couple of guys come and help my opponent out of the ring. I feel slaps on my back in congratulations and boasting. I'm too hyped up to think rationally. This is how guys get lost in this shit. The high of fighting is like nothing else. That guy is no Red, but he's a damn good fighter. Right now, all I can think about is pounding him to the ground, or anyone else who crosses my path.

"Kid, you did it. Here, drink this." He thrusts a Gatorade bottle in my hand and without thinking, I take a swig off it. It's ice cold water, and it helps. I swish and spit, getting the blood taste out of my mouth. My eyes settle on Tomlin and he's grinning from ear to ear. "Come on, I want you to meet someone."

We make our way through the crowd. The mix of anger and excitement washes over people's faces, depending on who they bet on. What I do notice in my somewhat Neanderthal fog is that these are people I know. Well, know of, or have seen before. Then I come face to face with Atticus Kleinfeld.

I can't help myself, my eyes go wide. So do his, but that's beside the point. I'm fairly certain I'm made, and this whole operation is going to go up in smoke. Fuck, how do I get out of this?

"Mr. Tomlin, who do I have the pleasure of meeting?"

"This, sir, is Thatcher. He's the kid Miles recruited in the Santa league."

"Thatcher? Don't I know you from somewhere?" He sticks his hand out to shake and I take it firmly, shaking in return. There is a test of strength there and by the look on his face, I'm going to win it.

"Not that I know of, sir. But I get that a lot. I have one of those faces." I'm hoping beyond hope he buys that. Or, at least plays along. But if he's here, and Tomlin's calling him sir, Elle's going to need to know. He definitely has the money to back this kind of operation.

"My mistake," he smirks. "Mr. Tomlin speaks highly of you. After tonight's performance, I see why. Looked like you were favoring your right side out there."

"Nothing I can't handle, sir." I play it off, but holy fuck do I hope there is not another fight next weekend.

"Great to hear! I guess that means you'll be entering him into the Christmas event, Charles?"

I keep my face neutral and watch Mr. Tomlin for his response. I'm groaning internally.

"You bet. Kid's a gold mine. Plan to finally knock you off your North Pole trophy."

Both men laugh and we part ways.

I was hoping to get dressed and head out, anxious to get to Elle and tell her what happened. Though, after seeing the car tailing me, that might be a terrible idea. Fuck, I hate this undercover shit. I want to just call the captain and have them round all these fuckers up. Not only is there illegal fighting, there are definitely drugs. The men openly snorting what I can only imagine is cocaine of their tables don't even care who sees them. But I don't get to do any of the things I want to do tonight. Tomlin's on me like paper to glue. He shows me around and introduces me to so many people I can't even remember half their names.

He is definitely parading his prize cock. There is a lot of bluster about Christmas Eve. I keep my face calm, but I'm pretty worried about the whole thing. I can't even lift my arm right now with how badly it hurts. Every one of these assholes shakes my hand, and it sends pain radiating through my chest. I get a beer, and I watch the bartender pop the top then hand it to me. When I go to pay, he waves me off and I shrug. I'm not asking twice.

After an hour of socializing, I'm drawn into a lively game of poker. Again, I'm gifted something. They float me the chips to play. I'm shit at poker, especially on my third beer, and now distracted with the pretty little thing in my lap. She smells sweet, and to look at her, she's pretty enough. I have a sneaking suspicion she costs a fortune. I am content to let her sit in my lap, pet her, and let her pretend to accidentally brush against my dick when she squirms. I'm fairly sure she is helping the other men cheat.

Atticus Kleinfeld is watching me every time I look up. His expression looks like a cross between bemused and suspicious. I give him a nod and tip my beer at him. His grin broadens and I'm the first to look away as I have to focus on the game. "Fuck, again? I have the worst luck," I grumble as I throw my cards down.

"Awe, sweety. Why don't you give me a kiss for luck? Maybe you'll win the next hand."

I let her kiss me. It's clinical, and she tastes of stale cigarettes, killing any potential hard-on I might have gotten from kissing her. She looks smug and I take a swig of my beer to quickly wash away that taste. Boy, do I miss Elle's sweet mouth right now. Her lucky kiss goes over about as well as I suspected it would, and I lose the hand, losing the last of my chip pile.

"Well, gents, and lady, it has been fun. But it's time for this pumpkin to pumpkin." I wait for her to get up, before I do, and she pouts at me.

"Awe! Thought maybe we could get a little nightcap, champ." If I leave with her, who knows what will happen.

"Sorry, darlin'. I gotta get home to my ol' lady. She's already gonna kill me for bein' late."

It works, and I'm able to head out. The drive home feels like it takes hours longer than it really does. By the time I come stumbling into my apartment, it's close to eight in the morning. The apartment is quiet, and I don't want to disturb Meg. I make a beeline for my bedroom and quietly close the door behind me. One hot shower, two painkillers, and a large glass of water later, I am sitting on my bed upset that being horizontal hurts more than sitting. I mutter as I make my way to the old recliner in the living room. It takes a few minutes to situate myself and throw a blanket over me as I pull up the recliner. It's not long before I am out cold.

## CHAPTER TWENTY-FOUR

### *Santa Wolfe Is on His Way*

I wake to someone banging on my door. Then I hear the door open. It's enough to make me come up out of the chair, ready to box, even if the sudden movement makes me grit my teeth. I am not greeted with anything nefarious. Well, she might be nefarious if you ever anger her enough, but right now, she looks irritated, not nefarious.

"Elijah Joseph, why are you naked in your — What has happened to you? Do I need to call your father?"

"What? No, Ma, what are you doing here?"

"Non. You are going to tell me what is going on with you this instance. What have you been doing that you are beaten and bruised? I went by the police station to deliver your cookies, and they told me you have not been to work for weeks."

"Fuck, Ma, really? You took my cookies to the office?" I groan as I grab the blanket and wrap myself before I stalk into my bedroom.

She does not follow me, thankfully, but I hear the fridge door open. It makes me smile that even though I'm a grown ass man she still checks to see if I am stocking my fridge with something other than beer. I get dressed quickly and come back out to find her sitting at the dining room table, her hands resting neatly in her lap.

"Assez-vous," she chirps, but I know better than to argue. So, I sit in the chair she had pushed from under the table with her foot. I am bracing myself for a barrage of questions that I can't answer. They don't come. She stares at me, her face drawn into her disapproving frown. I take in the vision of my mother, and guilt fills me.

"Maman, I'm sorry. I can't talk about it right now. I've been so busy I didn't think to tell you I wasn't going to be in the office." I feel like she just caught me and Janey Gates the night I popped her cherry. I rub my hand over my face.

"Joseph," her tone is soft. "I do not like zhis." Before I can move out of reach, she takes a hold of my chin with those perfectly manicured nails and turns my face to inspect it. "You are a good boy, and you are acting like a thug."

"Ma, it's not like that," I grumble.

"Oh? You are stringing along two women. Lying to your parents. You forgot our shopping trip yesterday. You have not been to work in two weeks, and I find you beaten in your recliner. What exactly is it like?" Her French accent makes her sharp words sound even harsher than she means.

"I'm not stringing two women along," I sound twelve.

"Oh? I very well know you are not engaged to that Harris girl. Yet, her mother is convinced the two of you are. Then you still have that girl," she motions to Meg's room, "living with you. Just what do you think you are doing? You are not one of those swinger people, are you?"

I cannot stop the blush that creeps over my cheeks. "I… We're not… Meg's just a friend, Maman."

"Uh-huh. Friends do not have sex with each other, Joseph."
She gives me another pointed look.

"Depends on the friend," I try to defend myself only to see
the mix of anger and surprise cross her face.

"Hrmph," is the reply I get. Why do women make this
sound? It's not helpful other than to tell me I gave her the
wrong answer. She sighs. "Get your shoes on, you are coming
with me."

I start to protest. I just want to relax and do nothing
strenuous for a few days. I wish I could tell her I'm on a case.
But the last thing I want is to get her involved in this Santa
League bullshit. So, I get up and get my shoes, like the good
son I am, and we head out.

That woman keeps me out all day. But it is nice to spend
some quality time with Maman. Even when angry, she is a
pleasure to be around. I swear we enter every shop in the mall
looking for gifts. I have to resist the urge to step into a lingerie
shop, but Maman would frown if I only buy enough for one
woman in my life and read me the riot act if I buy enough for
two. I do struggle with carrying all her bags for her, but I'm
too stubborn to let her carry any of them. We stop by the
house, and I am glad my younger brother, Jean-Luc, takes
most of the bags. By the time she drops me off at home, I am
exhausted and it's after sundown.

I show up for training the next morning at five o'clock.
Only, my trainer apparently didn't get that memo. I spend
three hours puttering around the gym, taking it easy due to
my injuries. I don't want them to see that I'm really in no
shape to fight on Wednesday, so when he shows up at eight,
he gives me the most lightweight pansy-ass training routine I
have ever been through. Then, as if to pour salt in the wound,

he is done at eleven. I don't argue about the merits of Red's full day workouts, as I'm hurting pretty badly. I'm also pretty sure Gavin's a huckster put in place to set me up to fail. Not by Tomlin, as Tomlin very much gains from my winnings. Then again, I thought Miles did, too. Honestly, I don't care.

I call Elle's office phone from a pay phone, and it just rings. That's odd. She should be at the office right now. Then again, she might be out working some angle I don't know. So, I pick up some of Meg's favorite fast food, and head home.

"Honey, I'm home," I joke when I walk through the door. It's quiet, so she might still be asleep. She is usually up and out of bed by one in the afternoon. I set our lunch down on the table and head over to her room. The door is slightly open, so I knock. "Hey, hot stuff, brought you lunch." The door swings open with an eerie squeak and the first thing I notice is the complete disarray of her room. Meg's a bit of a neat freak, and her room is always kept tidy.

I push the door open fully to see a ransacked, hot mess, as if a hurricane came barreling through. "Meg," I call louder. My heart is in my throat as my trained eye starts to pick through the details of the mess. I carefully make my way to her bathroom, but it is all in order. I come back to the room and hesitate. I should call the cops and get the boys down here to treat this like a crime scene. Then I see a piece of paper on the bed.

I pick it up and I read, *Throw the fight on Wednesday if you want the girl back. Don't fuck this up, Thatcher.*

I stare at the note and narrow my eyes. "No, that fuck wouldn't," I try to convince myself. I stalk out of the bedroom and into mine. It takes a few minutes to find the jacket with the bet slip in it, but I unfold it and bring it up next to the other. "That fuck," I growl. I stuff both pieces of paper into my jeans pocket and I tear out of my apartment like a man on fire.

My first stop is the Wooden Nickel. I shove open the door and head straight for the bartender. "Where is he?"

"Where the fuck is who, Thatcher?"

"Miles. Where the fuck is that prick?"

He moves for the shotgun under the bar and I'm over it faster than lightning. He gets it out of the rack, but I have him disarmed and have it aimed at him, cocked and ready to shoot. I wouldn't, but he doesn't need to know that.

"Tell me where the fuck he is, or I swear to God I'll—,"

"What the fuck is going on out here?" I look from the bartender to the woman who appears, Alicia. "Thatcher? What the fuck do you want?" She does not appear to be the least bit afraid of me pointing a shotgun at her husband. "I told you that thing was more trouble than it's worth!" She whacks his arm, and I would grin at how cute they are together, if I weren't so fucking pissed that Miles has done something to Meg.

"This way," she jerks with her head and motions for me to follow her to the back.

I walk her husband back with the shotgun until I can follow her, taking my chances with my back to her over him. Once we are through the door to the back of the top-level bar, I lower it, and turn to face her. She takes a seat in a closet-sized room.

"What the fuck do you want with Miles?"

"This," I fish out the crumpled papers and toss them onto her desk.

She carefully picks them up and opens the larger of the two.

I see her brows raise, then she closes the paper. She scribbles something on the larger paper and hands it back to me. "Get the fuck out of here. I'm not telling you shit. And if I see you here again, I'm callin' the cops."

I pick up what she is putting down and I throw my fist into the wall for show, while also turning to leave. I keep the shotgun. Damn fool doesn't know how to use it, anyway. I toss it into the trunk of the shitty sedan, and I take off for the address given.

## CHAPTER TWENTY-FIVE
### *I'll Be Home For Christmas*

I spend the rest of the day fuming in my loaner car. I set myself up so I could watch his house. Miles lives in one of these fancy housing additions they have recently built. Manicured lawn, two-car garage, that he parks in, and one big picture window. I have seen no sign of Meg yet, but I'm figuring they are keeping her in a bedroom somewhere. They order pizza and Miles answers the door. That prick doesn't look worried in the least. I hope they haven't hurt Meg. I would never forgive myself if she got mixed up in this.

Then there is a tap on the window.

I look up, and of course it's the county sheriff. I roll the window down, "Hey, Jim. Can't really talk right now."

"Wolfe, what the fuck are you doing way out here? Got a couple o' housewives spooked about some guy creeping around the neighborhood."

"Look man, unless you plan to be back-up I really can't be chit-chatting. I'll head around the block."

"Yeah. Well, whatever you're doin', these hens'll be all over you. Don't make me have to come talk to your mug again. And tell your uncle he owes me money."

I laugh, and then it dawns on me. "I will. But you could always tell him yourself as you regale him with how you had to bail my ass out."

"What are you playin' at, Wolfe?"

"So, I'm kind of workin' something here, and I'm struggling with how to solve the problem."

"What's that got to do with me?"

I fish the note from my pocket and hand it over to him. He raises a brow at me as he cracks it open. His expression darkens, and I know exactly where his mind went.

"I'm listenin'." His entire demeanor changes, and if he were a dog, he would be on point.

"Asshole that took her, and the girl are in that house right there. You up for a little razzle dazzle?"

"I think that could be arranged."

"One catch. You gotta bowtie 'em for the feds."

"What the fuck are you doing working for the feds? Can't those lazy pricks get their own shit done?"

"Trust me, I understand. But that idiot decided to cross the river. So, if you'd be so kind."

"Awoo."

"Awoo." I respond with a grin. "And I promise to not scare anymore housewives."

I watch as Jim shakes his head and moseys back to his car. It'll probably take them an hour or two to get things moving, but at least I can trust Meg will be alright. I don't have to sit around and ride his ass. Jim's one of my uncle's buddies. While my uncle was KCPD, he and Jim worked together to not only find my sister-in-law, Franky, but to bring her home. The way my uncle tells it, it's the only time he ever saw Jim come to tears.

I take off, like I've been run off by that cop and I head to home. I don't collect two hundred dollars. I park my ass in my dining room and wait. About three hours later, my apartment becomes a three-ring circus as it's crawling with Feds. I furrow my brow as Agent Harris isn't among them. I think that's odd, but then here comes Frank. He has murder in his eyes, and he pulls me aside while the rest of his team gets to work.

"You Thatcher?" He barks the question even though he damn well knows who I am.

"Yes, sir."

He glances over his shoulder and ushers me further into my galley kitchen where he can watch all the other fed rats running around while he talks to me. "You wanna tell me what the fuck is going on?"

"The man that got me into this underground shit, got mad I won. He took the girl to force me to throw the next fight."

Frank pinches the bridge of his nose, and I can read his body language. Something isn't right. Then he sighs and rubs his face. "Get a go bag for the two of you and get the hell out of here."

"I ain't leaving until the hospital calls me."

"She's at County General. The next time you have an update, you call my desk."

I frown at that. Why doesn't he want me to call Agent Harris? I start to ask that very question, but I can read the look on his face. I shut my trap and do what I was told to do.

I hotfoot over to County General and Meg's docile. My guess is they gave her something to calm her down. She buries herself against my chest and I hug her tight.

It doesn't take us long to get to the safe house, and I get her settled in one of the guest rooms. I feel like shit, and I struggle to get comfortable on the bed in the room next to hers, before I finally fall asleep.

It's still dark when I feel the weight on my bed. I crack my eye open, and I frown when I see Meg crawling under the blanket as she curls right to me. She is trembling. I don't say a word to her. I put my arm around her and pull her close to me.

"I'm sorry. I... It's just... I was in bed when... he--."

I hear the hitch in her voice.

I now know how my brother must have felt when he finally got his wife back. I only had a day or two of that helpless feeling of Meg being taken. He lived for months with that feeling. Then to have her trembling, and now crying, against me I pull her tighter. I don't love Meg like that, but if I could murder Miles for what he has done to her, I would. "I got you. You're safe."

"What if he comes back?"

"He ain't comin' back, Meg. I promise." I clench my jaw because protocol dictates I keep quiet.

"You can't know that. And he said... if you didn't do what he wanted he would make sure to..." She clings tighter, forcing my breath to hitch as she compresses my ribs, and my heart breaks. That fucking prick has stolen her right from me.

"Meg. I'm gonna tell you something. Then we're gonna get some sleep. After that, you're going to call your Ma, alright? I think it's time you two talked."

"Joe, I don't know. She's just gonna yell and scream about how I'm a no-good whore who does the devil's work."

"She's still your mamma. And if she's as hard-nosed as you say, you can always spend Christmas with Maman. Now, I know for a fact, Miles ain't coming around anymore. The FBI took him, and they can't let him go until after I'm off the case."

"But what about after?"

"Well, call it a Christmas miracle, but I won't be off this case before Christmas. Which gives you enough time to breathe. I got you."

"Awoo?" It's so fucking cute I grin at her chirping my family's callsign to me.

"Awoo," I grunt at her, which makes her giggle like a small child.

"Now, get some sleep." I kiss her forehead and I adjust so she is not crushing my ribs, so we can nestle down together.

I can't sleep for long as the pain from my injuries pulls me out of slumber. Not to mention, I got used to Red's ass-crack of dawn shit show. I see Meg all curled up, and cute in her sleep. While I'm not sleeping, I stay here and hold her, my hand gently petting down her spine. I'll give her this extra time to rest, as I feel guilty that she needs it at all. It's about nine in the morning when she finally rouses.

"Mornin', sunshine." I wink.

"I could get used to waking up to that smile. Gonna make me breakfast too, Wolfe?"

"So demanding. I suppose," I mock sigh as I ease out of the bed. "Call your ma."

"Jerk," I hear her mutter as I head into the kitchen.

She follows me and picks up the phone on the wall. I rummage through the fridge, gathering up the food to make omelets, silently thanking Elle for stocking food. I listen as Meg talks with her mother, but I don't interject. Meg gets about two words in before she's a blubbering mess. I glance in her direction and hand her a paper towel for the tears. If her mother's reading her the riot act, we're going to have words.

Thankfully, that is not what happens. She quietly hangs up the phone about the time I am flipping her omelet over.

"Well?" I ask her without looking up.

"She asked me to come home."

"You gonna go?"

"Yeah, Joe. I think I am gonna go. At least for a few weeks."

# CHAPTER TWENTY-SIX

## *It Came Upon a Midnight Clear*

*December 13*

Elle stands in the kitchen of the safe house. Her arms are crossed, and her foot is tapping in irritation. Joe should have been here by now. That was their agreement. He fights the fight and then comes and informs her of what he has learned for the week. Only now he isn't here. She glances at her watch again and it says one-fourteen. "Fucking Wolfe," she mutters.

Then the phone rings.

"What?" she growls into the receiver.

"He ain't comin'. He went home with the redhead."

"Hrmph," she grunts and hangs up the phone. Elle doesn't want to admit to herself she is jealous. It's not like they're a thing. He's not actually her fiancé. She is pissed he is fucking around when he should report in. That's what she tells herself when she snatches up her car keys and storms out.

By the time she gets home, she's still not over Joe standing her up. She hrmphs, and she manages her feelings the way every jilted woman in her position does, with a bottle of red wine. About halfway through the bottle, "If he can fuck, so can I," and she picks up the phone. It takes a moment, but she dials Gideon's number.

"Hello," his voice thick from sleeping.

"I'm halfway through a bottle of red. You better be here before I finish it." She then hangs up the phone.

When Gideon arrives, she has been through the first bottle and part of the way through a second. "You're late. I had to open the second bottle. Now get naked. I want to fuck."

"Yes, ma'am," Gideon smirks as he steps into her humble abode. He's in sweatpants and a t-shirt. It doesn't take long for him to strip down before the glass of wine hits the floor, and she's stripped of her clothing as well.

With an easy motion, Gideon bends her over the back of her couch and parts her legs like he's going to frisk Elle. He reaches up with one hand and laces his fingers into her hair, pulling her head back to force her to arch as he teases his head against her.

"Don't tease, just fuck," she whines.

He slaps her ass with the other hand, "Be quiet. I'll tease you if I want to and you'll like it." He then thrusts into her once, letting her squirm and get used to him before he obliges and pumps into her roughly. He uses the hold on her hair to give him extra leverage as he drives into her.

Elle moans and pushes back against him. It doesn't take long before he is shuddering against her, blowing his load deep. She isn't satisfied though and as he eases from her, she lifts and turns, essentially pulling him over the couch onto the cushions. She follows him over the edge and her hot wet mouth engulfs his head to suck him hard again.

"Holy fuck, Elle," he moans. His eyes roll into the back of his head, and he happily pets her, trying to hold her head in place as she successfully brings him back to life. He gasps when she lets him pop from her mouth. He isn't left hanging long as she crawls up him the rest of the way and without warning mounts him. His eyes grow wide in fascination as she rides him like a bucking bronco. His eyes follow her bouncing breasts as she leans back and lifts her hands into the air to just enjoy the ride.

How could he deny such a beautiful thing? He rests his hands on her hips and thrusts for all he's worth up into her. His breathing is labored, and their bodies shimmer from their efforts until she finally shudders on him, milking his already throbbing cock. It draws forth a second load. "That," he breathes, "was amazing."

She collapses down on him and brings a finger to his lips. "Shh. Don't talk. You'll ruin it." This makes him smirk, and he settles onto the couch more, wrapping an arm around her to keep her from falling off as he feels his cock still pulsing in her.

They had drifted to sleep at some point, so the phone ringing wakes Elle enough to whine, "No. Don't wanna." Gideon, ever the gentleman, rotates them enough to free himself of her, causing her to whine when he pops free. He chuckles and then staggers to the phone.

"Hello," Gideon says as he watches the adorable figure of Elle curled up on her couch naked.

"Who is it?" she grumbles from the couch.

"Put Elle on," the man's voice barks at Gideon. He wonders who would call Agent Harris in the middle of the night. Then again, she called him in the middle of the night, and he came running.

"It's for you, he sounds angry." Gideon watches as Elle stumbles off her couch and with wobbly legs makes her way to him.

"Hello?" Her voice is sleepy sounding.

Gideon stays close, watching as Elle goes from sleepy afterglow to poker-faced agent in no time flat.

"None of your fucking business, what do you want?" Her voice was no longer that sultry sleepy sound and holding a menacing promise of tearing whoever was on the other end a new asshole. Then silence again. She is watching Gideon purposely without answering for several beats.

"Thanks, I'll take care of it," then she hangs up and frowns. She hadn't told Gideon why he was there. She just happily got lost in a bottle of wine and then taking the thorough fucking he gave her.

"Everything alright?" he asks Elle as she frowns at him.

"It's fine. You need to go."

"Anything I can do to help?"

"No," Elle hesitates, "it's personal." She likes Gideon, but this past week of researching finances and paperwork has revealed a pattern to her that suggests this has been going on for some time and those on the inside of the law have been turning a blind eye. So, while she would love to tell Gideon all about Joe, she felt it prudent to keep her informant safe.

"Was that your boyfriend?"

"Ex. Needs me to help his sister." She lies outright and then turns to get dressed.

Gideon watches her for a moment before he gathers his belongings to get dressed as well. He could tell she isn't telling him everything, and from his own experiences no one rushes out to help the sibling of an ex like that. But he lets it go. For whatever reason, she isn't willing to let him in on it. He does pull her into a heated kiss. "You owe me, Harris."

"I owe you?" Elle chuckles. "If I remember correctly, counselor, the mess on my couch would suggest you were well satisfied. So, if anybody owes anybody, you owe me." She leans up and pulls him into another kiss. "Now get out of here," swatting his ass. She waits until she sees his car pulling away before she finishes getting dressed.

It doesn't take Elle long to get to the hospital and take over the chaos that is a young girl being brought in by a young man that no one seems to be able to track down. There is at least that. She didn't want them seen together at this point of the case, even if it's in passing. She gets everything squared away with the hospital administration to make sure all lab work and other information is handed over to the FBI for the case and she heads into Red's room.

She takes a seat next to the redhead and starts to flip through the channels on the television. It's early in the morning, and as tired as Elle is, she imagines this girl is pretty important to the case, or Joe wouldn't have bothered. It's hard for her, looking at the girl, she feels the ugly dragon of jealousy rearing its head. Joe went home with her. He has been flirting heavily with this girl from the get-go. Elle leans forward on her knees, trying to decide why she even cares.

"Who the feck are you?" Red pipes up several minutes later.

"I'm your fucking fairy godmother, that's who."

"Why the feck do I need a fairy godmother? All I need is a dram of whiskey and a plane ticket."

"That so? Well, Shannon Mallory, it would appear you are in a lot of trouble."

"The feck I am? Why am I in a hospital?"

"A man brought you in, said you passed out on him and quit responding."

Elle watches as Red's freckly face scrunches up in thought then responds with, "Thatcher brought me here? Who the feck are you again?"

The doctor comes in before Elle can respond. He is looking over the chart and starts to speak to Red when he sees Elle. "Who are you?" the doctor frowns at Elle.

She sighs and stands, bringing her FBI ID out of her pocket. "I'm Agent Harris, and I am the lead on this case. What did the labs say?"

# CHAPTER TWENTY-SEVEN
## *Go Tell It on The Mountain*

There is a brief pause in the room and Elle can feel the tension rising. The dirty look from Shannon and the pensive worry from the doctor made Elle sigh internally.

"We found traces of quaaludes in her system. While there was not enough to actually threaten her life, had she been brought in any later, we might not have gotten them at all."

Elle watches as the doctor checks over the girl. "I'll get all the paperwork started for your release. Try to stay out of trouble." He then heads out of the room for his rounds. This leaves Elle to turn and face the young girl in the bed. The girl's face is scared and pale, the realization that she has been drugged is enough to rattle her. She takes her seat next to the bed and leans back, crossing her arms. "You have two choices, kid. One, you play dumb and don't cooperate. Then you go to prison with the rest of them. Or two, you cooperate, and we talk about how you get out of this situation."

"Feck off. I'm the victim here. You can't arrest me fer bein' drugged."

"I can't? From where I sit, you partook of illegal substances gained during other unlawful activities. I could have your passport revoked, citizenship scrutinized, and drop you into a deep dark hole where the only people who know you exist would rather you didn't. Want to try your luck at that? I'm not the boys at the gym you can flirt and flounce your way out of trouble with."

Fear washes over Shannon's face as Elle plays hard ball. She looks down at her hands and chews against her lip. Elle realizes this girl isn't more than nineteen, twenty years old, and her irritation with Joe even flirting with her grows. Elle wants to tell the girl she's safe and that it's a bluff. That her life will be ten times easier if she cooperates, and that Joe is the one who brought her here, keeping her safe. The girl still hasn't confirmed to Elle she's not one of them. For all Elle knows, this is a ruse to flush out Joe.

"Ya won't hurt Thatcher, will ya?" Shannon looks up with those big doe eyes to Elle, and Elle has to restrain herself from rolling hers. Of course, that's the first thing the girl worries about.

"I think you should worry about yourself, kid. I'm sure this Thatcher can take care of himself. That who brought you in?"

"I don't know. He's the last thing I remember from last night. And I know he didn't give 'em to me."

"Then who did? Listen kid, I'm on your side. I want to help you, but you have to give me something to do that. My hands are bound by the law."

Shannon snorts then, and it makes Elle raise a brow. Elle can see the suspicion and fear etched on the girl's face. This girl has been a fighter for a long time, and to be hung up by the law now is not sitting well with her. "The law's in on it. For all I know, you're one o' theirs. And I'm fucked no matter the way I go."

Elle softens a little as her suspicions are confirmed about people on the inside being involved. She rubs her hand over her face and sighs as she tries to decide how to work this girl into turning to their side. "I know you're probably scared. I can help you. Come with me to the federal building and we'll work out a deal where you get what you want, and we put these fucks away. So they don't do it to someone else."

Okay, it's cheesy, and Elle knows it. She also knows deep down, people want to be the big damn hero. She imagines this girl is no different.

"Looks like I don't have much of an option, now do I?"

"I'm afraid not."

The conversation dies off there, and Shannon is brought hospital scrubs for pants, and given her t-shirt back. A pair of canvas slip-on shoes are supplied and Elle escorts her out of the hospital in cuffs. Joe's behavior told her the hospital is being watched, and she wanted to give the show that she had 'captured' Shannon, not coerced her into helping. They show up at the federal building and she puts her into an interrogation room with breakfast and a cup of coffee.

Elle heads into Frank's office and closes the door behind her while he is on the phone. She is making a show of wanting privacy for this conversation as she then turns his blinds so the rest of the office cannot see them talking, either. She takes a seat across from him and silently waits for him to finish his call.

"I'll call you back, Henderson." He hangs up the receiver and raises a brow at Elle. "What now, Harris?"

"Wolfe bow-tied us an eyewitness if we can flip her."

"Oh? You know I have been on the phone all morning with the suits. Seems they are eager to move forward on this case.

Assigned us a prosecutor to help expedite everything. You wouldn't know anything about that, would you?"

"No, of course not, sir," Elle flashes him a grin. "I may have made a friend at the courthouse."

"Uh-huh. I don't want to know. Tell me about the witness."

"It's the girl from the gym. The trainer. Name's Shannon Mallory. Wolfe said he thought she might have been forced in, and last night he called me to pick her up at County General."

Frank's face scrunches in concentration, and he says nothing for several beats. His expression makes the hair on the back of Elle's neck raise. He finally exhales dramatically before he leans forward. "Look. You need to get her to flip, or we have to put Wolfe on the case files."

"Wait. He's not on the files? I filed the paperwork-."

"I know what you did, Agent Harris. I stalled the paperwork on Wolfe. Your gut was right to not trust people. Listen, I'm following some leads of my own, so I need you to handle the girl and to keep Wolfe out of it as much as possible. From all the people on my ass about you working this case, it sounds like we're onto something big. Don't fuck it up."

"Yes, sir," Elle eases up and turns to leave.

"Oh, and Harris," Frank chimes when she's halfway out the door. He waits for her to look back. "You fuck in the conference room again and you're fired." He flashes her a grin.

By the time Elle walks back into the interrogation room, the pink has faded from her cheeks. She's holding her own cup of coffee in one hand, with a stack of case files in the other. The room is a drab gray color with a metal table bolted to the floor, three chairs of nondescript gray, the standard big mirror window, along with the blaring white light from the ceiling. Elle settles into the chair and sips her coffee without opening the file yet.

"I'm not tellin' you shit until I get a deal."

"What do you want in this deal?"

"My money. No jail time. And to go back to Ireland. And..." Shannon hesitates and her cheeks blush. She shifts in her seat and looks from Elle to the mirror behind her. "And for Thatcher to not get in trouble."

"Tell me about Thatcher. Must be some catch that you'd hang your freedom on the line for him." Of course, Joe would have wooed her in this short of a while. He must have a super-powered dick. It only serves to irritate Elle more thinking about him fucking this girl.

"Thatcher's a dirty feckin' liar. He fights like military an' he lies like a four-year-old. Don't know if he works for you, or what, but he ain't no down-on-his-luck wannabe fighter. And... well... If they find that out about him, he'll never get out alive."

Elle watches as Shannon sulks and frowns. Then kicks herself for spilling the beans on Thatcher without getting what she wants. Behind the mirror, unknown to Elle stands Gideon and Frank.

"Is Thatcher one of ours?" Gideon asks Frank.

"No," Frank lies. Until Elle tells him Gideon's on the up and up, he's not spoiling any of her case for her. No matter how squeaky clean this kid appears to be on paper.

"Sounds like a regular prince charming, Shannon, but this Thatcher's not in the hot seat. You are. If he's as goody goody as you say he is, he'd tell you to worry about yourself, and not him. I can't get you a deal without something to show you're willing to work with us. It's not just a statement. You'll have to testify, and I can't promise no jail time if what we find says you're a criminal too."

"Then why the feck would I tell you anything? If you had somethin', you wouldn't need me to sing like a bird. Yer fishin' and I'm no' a snitch."

"No. You're the girl they drugged with quaaludes so you wouldn't remember what happened to you. Or worse, wouldn't put up a fight when they did whatever they intended." Elle lays out the outcome she has put together for last night's festivities. She half-heartedly wishes Joe had given her more information, but it's not stopping from her drawing the picture for Shannon to make her own conclusions. The girl's responses tell Elle as much about what they are dealing with as witnessing it would.

"Feck," she whines and kicks the table leg. "Feck! Feck! Feck!"

Elle stays cool as a cucumber and sips her coffee, letting the younger girl get it out of her system.

"Fine. I know it all. I know how they work, who they are, where they operate, and who they all answer to here. I'm not sayin' shit until I get the deal."

"Fair enough. I'll be back." Elle stands, taking the file with her.

# CHAPTER TWENTY-EIGHT
*Getting Nuttin' for Christmas*

Elle left the interrogation room and is met with Gideon and Frank. Her brow quirks at Gideon being present, but the calm posture of Frank tells her he is okay with the man being in on the conversation. The silent look between Frank and Elle says they both hate dealing with lawyers and deals. They would much rather just put the bad guys away and let the rest of them sort it out. Frank takes them back to his office to keep as few people involved as possible.

"It'll take me a few days to get a deal." Gideon says. "I have to run it up the chain. I can tell you now, the money is off the table. But the rest we can work on."

"The longest we can hold her is forty-eight hours without her cooperation."

"Well, then it looks like I need to get to work," he winks at Elle. "Hope all that shit with your ex worked out."

Once he's gone, Frank eyes Elle. "Really? Are you fucking serious, Harris?"

"What?" She feigns innocence.

"Look, I don't give a fuck about how much of a whore you

want to be outside of work. That's your business. But you are bringing that shit into my house. First Wolfe, now him. You don't want to be pegged the girl that fucks her way through the office."

"Fuck you, Frank. The only reason I have that reputation is you let those assholes spread shit about you and me."

"Watch yourself, Harris."

"No. You watch yourself. I'm a good fucking agent who gets the job done. Who I fuck, and when I fuck them is none of your fucking business." Her voice raises considerably.

Frank stands and rests his hands on the desk, giving Elle the distinct impression of a silverback gorilla. "Noelle Harris, you watch your tone. I am your boss, not some boy you can string along. I am trying to help you. Get your head out of your ass and start acting like the agent I know you are. Now get the fuck out of my office."

Elle opens her mouth to retort, then clenches it closed. If she were a man, he would be patting her on the back for bagging so many chicks in such a fast turnaround. It's not fair, and she's sure Joe will get all the praise for his prowess in seducing Red. She fumes as she leaves the office. Spending the rest of the afternoon getting Shannon secured and safe for the time being. She opts to call in a few favors from retired officers as back-up to the official detail. These guys aren't even on the payroll, so they'll be able to blend in and intercept.

Once back at the office she starts going through the paperwork from the bank again. It's boring and dry research, but the patterns are starting to look obvious. As much as she wants to harass Wolfe, and share what she has found, he is in too deep for that. He would contact her. She finally heads home at about ten. It is probably the first good night's sleep she has gotten since this case started, and it's ruined by her mother storming her apartment at seven the next morning.

"Mom, I have to work."

"No. Take the day off. You and I have to meet with people to plan your engagement party."

"That's not how it works. Mom. Can't we wait until after Christmas to deal with this. Joe and I aren't even ready for a wedding. We want a long engagement."

"It is how it works. Do I need to have your father call your superior to get you off work?"

"Yah. 'Cause that looks professional. Hi. Frank. Yah, today my baby isn't coming to work because her mother wants to plan the wedding that isn't happening for at least a year."

"A year?! Oh, Noelle, that is not acceptable. You will have a Summer wedding. In June. We'll book the cathedral, and you'll have red roses with pink magnolias."

"I hate the color pink."

"No, you don't. You love pink. You wore it to every dance."

"Because you made me. I have always hated pink."

"You're just being contrary to be contrary. Now get out of the bed and get a shower. I will deal with your *work*."

Elle growls but stumbles out of the bed and stomps into the bathroom. Her mother is insufferable. She slams the door closed and turns on the water to wait for it to get hot. Through the door she can hear the muffled sing-song voice her mother uses on people when she wants them to do something for her. All Elle hears is, "…You're the best, Frank. Thank you!"

Elle doesn't take long to shower, but remains hiding in her bathroom for a good thirty minutes while she debates the merits of telling her mother the truth about her engagement to Joe Wolfe. On the one hand, her mother is putting on the happy face, and is excited to share this with her. On the other hand, her parents read her the riot act about marrying below her. Her father had been furious, and even went so low as to call the Wolfe family a bunch of thugs with a political strong-arm.

Her mother, the more diplomatic lawyer of the two of them, is at least trying to pretend she is happy for Elle. Elle finally exits her bathroom sanctuary to find her mother has laid out a dress and set heels aside for Elle. "I'm capable of dressing myself, mother."

"You are doing a terrible job of it. Look at these clothes. Are you pretending to be a man?"

"Yes, that's it. I want them to believe that I am a man because I wear slacks and sensible shoes to the job where I might have to run down a criminal or fight with someone. Let me just whip out my super heels and skirt of justice to make the criminals bend to my will. Really, you're a lawyer."

"Yes, well, I don't own any slacks." She makes the hrmph noise and Elle feels her cheeks turning red with rage. Several heavy breaths later she is stalking to her dresser to fish out under garments.

Their first stop is the cathedral.

"You know he is Lutheran, right?"

"He'll just have to convert."

"Do you really think he'll convert? How many Wolfes you know are Catholic?"

Her mother frowns at her, "Noelle," her tone throws the warning that she is about to cross a line with this defiance.

"I haven't even decided if I want a church wedding." Elle crosses her arms. The priest soon joins them, and the conversation goes even worse as Elle begins to question the priest about the very items the Lutherans left the church for in Germany.

He patiently answers her questions and chastises Elle for her behavior. He informs both of them he will need to meet the young man and they would need to go through counseling before he could even consider allowing them to marry there.

Their next stop is the florist. True to her mother's word she is shown red roses and pink magnolias. Elle rolls her eyes. "I hate all of these. I want wildflowers, and bright colors. Let's get lilies."

"Lilies are the flowers of death, Noelle."

"I know, mother. It is the death of my life as I know it."

"You have always been so dramatic."

"I am not being dramatic. I mean. It is traditionally frowned upon for wives to sleep with other men." Elle bats her eyelashes at her mother.

The slap that rings across her face is enough to bring tears to Elle's eyes and her cheeks flame red from embarrassment. "You will not speak to me like you are in some locker room. You are better than that, Noelle Winifred Harris. You will take this seriously, or so help me, I... I..."

"Disown me? Leave me alone? Treat me like a human being and not some meat market steer that will make you millions by being bred well?"

Her mother slaps her again and Elle sucks in a sharp breath. The florist quietly gathers up the flowers and leaves the two of them alone to have this conversation.

"You know what, mother," Elle's voice is dripping with fury. "I have a real job, with real problems to solve. Where people depend on me putting the bad guys away. Just like you used to care about. Just like dad used to care about. I am good at what I do. I am damn good at what I do. And I don't want to be someone's wife. I don't want to be someone's trophy. I sure as shit don't want to march down the aisle in some fluff ball of satin and tulle with a vomit of pink and red everywhere because that's what *you* like. So, you know what? *You* marry Joe Wolfe. Or whatever rich, fucking prick you think is worthy of your love. Because I am done with trying to win your love. There is no fucking engagement. I made it up! I conned Joe Wolfe into lying to you just so your little meat market parade would fail!"

Elle leaves her mother standing in the florist, gaping like a cod fish, as she storms out.

# CHAPTER TWENTY-NINE
*It's Beginning to Look a Lot Like Christmas*

Elle is sitting in her cubicle on Wednesday, tapping her pencil in irritation against the desk. She hasn't heard one peep out of Gideon since they sent him to negotiate the deal. She has been at her desk since before seven. Joe isn't answering his phone either. She has not heard from him since he called her about the girl. She picks up the phone and calls down to the front desk.

"No, Agent Harris, he has not entered the building. I promise you'll be the first to know."

She glances down at her empty coffee mug and thrusts up out of her chair, snatching the empty *World's Greatest Daughter* mug. She hurries to catch the elevator and nearly sprints to the break room where she can watch the main entrance. Filling her mug with cream, sugar and coffee. Still trying to look casual, she leans against the wall enjoying the coffee concoction. It's a good twenty minutes before she sees him strolling in like he owns the place.

Gideon's hair is combed back, and his suit is pristine. He pauses long enough to sign the log, and she's at the desk with a second cup of coffee ready for him. The security guard is laughing at her as she takes Gideon by the arm and drags him to the elevator. He laughs and takes her offered coffee. "Happy to see you too, Agent Harris."

"Do you have my deal?"

"Deal? What deal? Agent Harris, what are you talking about?"

Elle narrows her eyes at him. "Don't fuck with me, Gideon. There is a lot riding on this case. Did you get the deal, or not?"

Gideon raises a brow, his expression still holding the amused look. "Now, now, manners, Agent Harris."

The elevator dings to deposit them on her floor and he takes her right into the interrogation watch room. "Give us a minute, fellas?" He smiles to the two men setting up for the interview with Miss Mallory. They grin at each other and clear the room.

"You realize they think we're fucking in here?" Elle crosses her arms and gives him a dirty look.

"And? Who's to say we aren't?" He eases closer.

"Nuh-uh. No way, buster. It's one thing to bend me over the conference table after hours. It's a whole other thing during the day in a room that doesn't lock. Where's the deal?"

"Rumor is, you are back on the market and that your mother is scheduling a party for after Christmas. Something happen between you and Elijah Wolfe?"

Elle takes pause, her hand resting on the doorknob. It's like Gideon shocked her with a cattle prod. She clenches her jaw and takes several deep breaths before turning around. The murderous look he receives makes him downright laugh. "I know... I know. I shouldn't laugh. But the look on your face. You're the talk of the town, Harris. There are quite a few men fawning over getting in good with your family."

Elle stalks forward and jabs a finger in his face. "And let me guess, you're one of them? Give me the fucking deal and get out." She hisses at him.

He stands up straighter, squaring his shoulders until he somehow has filled the room, and he backs her right to the door before he pins her to it. "No," his voice rumbles deep and demanding. "I have your deal, Agent. Don't worry. I want to invite you to the Governor's ball."

"No."

"Here me--. "

"No."

"It will--."

"I fucking said NO!"

"Well, then I suggest you run, because your mother has put you back on the auction block. And I'd like to think you showing up with someone to spite her would be right up your alley. Besides, I thought every girl enjoys dressing up in fluffy ball gowns."

"Just how is attending the Governor's ball with you going to spite my mother?"

Gideon flashes his smolder smirk and leans in close. "Because then she'll see you are still slumming' it with the good guys instead of the rich boys." He leans in close and nuzzles against her check. "Come on, Elle. Just one night of merriment and fun. We'll dance. We'll drink. We'll fuck wherever you want to fuck, then... if you're lucky, I'll cook you breakfast."

Elle can't help herself and she laughs at his rather crass request. "If I say yes, will you give me my fucking deal?"

"Mhmm. And a fluffy dress?"

"Fuck no, but I'll wear something appropriate."

"I suppose then," he sighs with all the dramatics he can muster as he reaches down to open his briefcase. Gideon eases back, and she throws open the door before pulling the door stop in place. He chuckles, pulling out the deal. "It's only for immunity. It's the best I could do."

"It's a start. Hey, Tom!" Elle steps out of the room, now ignoring Gideon. "Bring me Miss Mallory."

Tom nods and hurries away before Elle sees Frank round the corner like he is going to murder someone. He stops when he sees Elle in the hallway with paper in her hand and then sees Shannon behind her being escorted into the interrogation room. Elle spins on heel and follows the girl in. Soon Tom and his tech lackey are back in the observation room with Frank and Gideon.

"This isn't a social club, boy."

"I don't know what you're talking about, Frank."

Frank snorts and shakes his head. "You fuck up this case, and I swear the only thing you will lawyer is the high school debate team."

Gideon chuckles, and eases forward as Elle and Shannon talk. "You guys have volume on them?"

Tom reaches over and flips a switch, which causes Shannon's voice to fill the room.

"What the feck is this? Where's my money? And all the other shit I asked for?"

"You haven't given us anything to even warrant the immunity, Red," Elle counters.

"Oh, now it's Red? Yer a dirty feckin' liar. Just like the rest." She crosses her arms and sulks like a petulant child.

"Red. Look. If you give us something, we can go back to the negotiation table. Let's start with how you came to be a part of this."

"Santorro. My da owed him a lot o' money. He was a boxer in Dublin. One night, after the fight, he told me I was goin' to America with Miles and that I had to do what he said."

Gideon and Frank watch as Elle probes and prods Shannon to get her talking and telling her story. Elle takes notes, and circles back when Shannon tries to duck questions. She talks about how they told her she had to earn her keep. "Miles was going to just pawn me off on Max and his wife, but then Max lost in the fight. He hit the mat...and didn't get up." Shannon frowns.

"What was Max's last name?"

"Carter. Wife's Becky. Miles took me to the gym, where I met Fraser. He trained me to fight."

Frank rubs his hand over his face. "Jesus, she was just a kid."

"It starts with the Santa League at the Nickel. And I was the wonder-kid." Shannon keeps talking and Elle keeps taking notes. The two men watch in fascination as this one girl unravels the entire ring of the Wooden Nickel.

"And that's when I was introduced to the big leagues. If I were you, I would be lookin' inta Tomlin's finances. He actually owns the Nickel, not Santorro." Shannon tilts her chair back, looking very much the young girl she is. "But I'm no' saying shit more until I get the rest o' my deal."

Elle takes a moment to look over what she wrote and then to Shannon. "Thank you, Miss Mallory. You have been most helpful. I'll take the deal back and see what we can do."

"Right. I'll bet yer jus' goin' cut me lose, and then I'm a dead woman." Elle watches as Shannon gets escorted away by Tom before she makes her way to the observation door.

With a frown, she brandishes the deal. "Get her the rest of her asks. She handed us the entry level guys on a platter." She hands the file back to Gideon.

"Yes ma'am," he tucks the contract in his briefcase and quickly makes his way out. Once he is gone, she looks at Frank. With a jerk of his head, he motions down the hall. She follows and they are in his office again.

"Who's Tomlin?" Frank sounds grim.

"Not sure. It's the first I heard of him. She's got a hell of a lot more to say, Frank. You need to keep her safe. She's going to be the lynchpin to this case."

"Don't tell me how to do my job, Harris. Now get out of here and find out who the fuck Tomlin is."

"Yes, sir," she mock salutes, but doesn't stick around to get her ass reamed by him a second time this week.

# CHAPTER THIRTY

*Rockin' Around the Christmas Tree*

*December 20, 1986*

Elle has to laugh at herself being so flustered about what to wear to this party. It's not like she is into Gideon. He is nice and all, but there is a control streak that sings red flag to her. As in, he likes to be in control and has no qualms with using his strength to get what he wants. She has seen it twice now. After tonight, she's going to tell him he is in the no-fly zone.

She leans forward in the mirror to apply the mascara. She has a touch of eye-shadow in place and a complete application of Tantalize-Me-Red on her lips. The black lace bra and panties give way to silky black stockings. With the finishing touches of her make-up complete she wanders back to her bed. The red sequined gown cost more than any person should spend on a dress, but it is exactly what she wants for tonight. It's not the traditional fluffy ball-gowns with poofy sleeves, but a sleek design instead. It's off the shoulder and form fitted with a slit that goes higher than is appropriate, but she doesn't care. She wants to look sinful tonight. Too bad Joe won't see it. In fact, she has not heard from Joe all week.

Frank has been handling him while she interrogates

Shannon. Not to mention, she has been playing catch-up on the paperwork. It is not uncommon to not speak with her informant. She and Frank had talked about keeping all the notes about Joe's involvement to a minimum. Frank had already uncovered that there was someone on the inside of Kansas City PD not playing on the up and up, and neither of them wanted to put Joe in any added danger than he is in.

She slips the gown on and uses a wire hanger to zip up the back. It's a trick she learned from her mother. She gingerly steps into the black heels and gives herself a once over in the mirror. As if he had been waiting for just that moment, Gideon knocks on her door. Snatching up her clutch, she answers the door and smiles as he wolf-whistles at her.

"Damn, Agent Harris," he taps his chest like his heart is beating out of it and she chuckles. He holds the door open for her to his expensive sports car and they are off to the Governor's ball. The drive is pleasant, and Gideon takes his time getting to the party. "So, I was reading over the case notes and noticed that there is an informant listed. You have someone other than the redhead working on this case?"

Elle shrugs, "I would rather not talk about work tonight, if you don't mind. I mean, we are celebrating sticking it to my mother."

"Fair enough. Just thought I would make small talk."

"If you knew I was engaged, why did you fuck me?" Elle smirks as she gives him a side glance. It has been gnawing at her since Wednesday. He mentioned her mother putting her back on the auction block and that means he damn well knew she had told everyone she is engaged to Joe Wolfe.

"Didn't see a ring on your finger. And well, thought I'd persuade you to join my team. If he couldn't keep you, why not give it a go myself. I mean, you're hot as hell, Elle."

"Uh-huh. You know there is a pre-nup for any of the Harris money I am entitled to."

"Damn. Caught me again. Here, I thought I would whisk you off your feet and you'd give me your millions."

"My parents' millions. I make far less than that."

"Hey," he reaches over and places a hand on her knee. "I am only teasing you, Agent Harris. I don't know what happened between you and Wolfe, but I can only hope you don't let it taint our friendship." His smile puts her at ease and his hand is firm on her knee.

She smiles in return, resting her hand on his, but does not otherwise talk to him about her personal life, or the case.

They arrive at the party and the valet takes the keys from him as he helps her out of the car. "You are going to be the shining star tonight," he murmurs against her temple.

The museum has been adjusted to host music and dancing, along with refreshments. Christmas decorations have been strewn throughout, sprinkled between pieces of artwork. Their coats are taken into an office turned coat check. His hand rests at the small of her back as he guides her into the party. He only parts from her long enough to get them each a drink. By the time he returns, she is listening quietly to several young men arguing about the merits of a new law being implemented by the mayor. While this ball is called the Governor's ball, it has nothing to do with him as he is in Jefferson City. It is a charity ball that the governor used to attend, and the name just stuck.

Before Elle can interject her point of view, she is swept onto the dance floor by Gideon. They are laughing at how terrible the other ball-gowns look when she is whisked from his arms and into the arms of another young eligible rich man. Her eyes roll at Gideon, but she can see the jealous look in his eyes. She shrugs and keeps dancing. He doesn't own her.

Conversation falls along the lines of what happened between Joe and her, then to what she plans to do after she gets married. She doesn't even have to pay attention when responding because they are so predictable. She knew her father had money, but she had not realized just how prominent her family had become in her absence. It's infuriating that none of these men assume she will keep working for the FBI. She is about to knock the teeth out of her current partner when Gideon steals her away from the dance floor.

"Thought you could use this," he hands her a tumbler glass filled with whiskey.

"Mhmm," she smiles and downs it like a shot.

Gideon's eyes widen and he coughs lightly when he takes the glass back, setting it aside. A quick glance to the clock on the wall and she has been here for only an hour. With a sigh, she slides her hand into his arm, "Lead on, prince charming. I'm sure there are men you need to mingle with."

"You sound like it will murder you to socialize."

"It might," she grumbles. Her cheeks feel flush, and she chalks it to the alcohol as they meander into the crowd of tuxes to mingle.

"I'll protect you," he chuckles.

For another hour she listens as bankers, lawyers, and other well-to-dos talk about their futures and plans as if she did not even exist. She has enough decency to not ruin this for Gideon. Another drink is given to her, and she sips it thoughtfully while listening to Gideon talk about his future.

He smiles at her when talking about family and Elle realizes then she is not okay.

She smiles at him, but she hasn't said a word for nearly thirty minutes. Everything is warm and fuzzy, like a dull roar more than distinct voices. She is having a tough time remembering what Gideon just said. It brings a frown to her perfectly red lips. When a lull in the conversation happens, she finally chirps. "I think it is time for Cinderella to leave the ball."

"Gentlemen," Gideon excuses them and he begins to guide her out. They pause at the coat-check office while their coats are retrieved. "You okay?"

"Mhm-hmm. Jus' wanna go home." Her speech slurs, and she frowns more. Bringing one hand up she feels the flush in her cheeks, and she looks back into the party. She knows she has not had enough alcohol to make her this drunk.

"Let's get you home," he says as he helps her into her coat. Then he is guiding her outside to his waiting car. He helps her into the passenger seat and even leans in to buckle her in. Quickly moving around to the driver's side, he pulls out of the museum parking lot.

There is silence for several minutes while she leans against the window, the icy cold feeling good against her burning up cheek. "Hey, baby, listen. I really need to know the name of the informant you have."

She scrunches her face into a frown. Her brain is muddled, and his words sound warbled. Like he is talking through water. "What? I don' wanna talk about work." She pouts at him.

"I know, but it's super important, honey. I just need his name and I'll drop it."

"Why? You not workin'. Hey... Dis ain't my splace." She looks up at the large gates parting for them to drive up to a massive estate house.

"Please, Elle. Just a name, that's all I need." The car comes to a stop and Elle is then feeling the chilly night air as her door is opened.

"Did you get it?"

"No. Jesus, she looks like she's going to pass out. You said that stuff would just loosen her up."

Elle frowns as her seatbelt is undone, and she looks from Gideon to come face to face with Henrik Kleinfeld. "Gideon," she stammers out.

"I'll take it from here." Henrik scoops her out of the car.

# CHAPTER THIRTY-ONE
## *So This Is Christmas*

Gideon is not about to leave Elle alone with Henrik. He already knows Henrik's penchant for physical altercations. They have been friends since grade school. Henrik wants to be a mobster when he grows up and his father's money has allowed him to get away with anything he sets his mind to. He watches as Henrik carries Elle up the stairs with little effort and nudges open a door to one of the offices in this house.

He deposits her in the chair and Elle looks from Henrik to Gideon. Even in the state she is in, the look of betrayal cuts Gideon. If she had just given him the name, they wouldn't even be here. Gideon runs his fingers through his hair and moves closer to Elle.

"Please, just give me his name. I can't help you if you don't tell me." The desperation in his voice is real.

Henrik's on the other side of the room, pouring himself a drink and amping himself up.

Elle motions for Gideon to come closer, like she is going to whisper it to him. When he leans in, "Your mom," she slurs. Her hand pushes against his shoulder and he grimaces as he steps back. He glances at Henrik again and steps back even further.

Henrik comes back to Elle and looks her over. "I would hate to ruin such a pretty dress," as he hoists her up like a doll. She is struggling, but her body feels heavy and slow to her. It's like she is moving through water. The zipper being undone is the only sound in the room, causing the gown to then pool onto the ground.

Henrik deposits her back in the chair while he kicks the gown away. "None of this has to happen, Noelle, if you just give us the name of your guy. Then it's all just a bad dream." His back is to her as he is rummaging for something.

Elle cocks her head and is fighting closing her eyes. She can feel her heart racing, and the adrenaline pumping, but her body is not responding to it. How stupid she has been. It's so plain to her now that Gideon is working for them. Has he compromised the whole case? Are they going to kill her? Fuck, no one knows where she is. She didn't even bother to tell her mother she was attending this ball. She hears Henrik talk to her and she snorts. "You realize you're fucked, Kleinfeld?" Her words are slurred together and slow, but she is smirking. "Kidsnapping a fed for one," she holds up two fingers.

He chuckles as he turns back, and without warning slams his fist into her cheek.

She grunts and slumps in the chair a little, shaking her head to keep awake as she feels the harsh stick of duct tape against her wrists, soon followed by around her ankles. "At least Gideon bought me dinner first," she groans. Then a fist to her stomach knocks the wind right out of her.

"Shut up. The only words out of your mouth should be the name of the guy working for you. Now, who is he?"

She narrows her eyes and says nothing.

He throws another punch to her gut.

She stays quiet. Her head lolls to look in the direction Gideon went. He is still there, his arms crossed and a grimace on his face. Another punch to her face makes her groan and turn her focus back to Henrik.

"Thought you said this broad was tough, Gideon? Look at her." He motions to Elle who does have tears in her eyes and her nose is starting to bleed. Her face feels like it's on fire and she closes her eyes, feeling the desire to go unconscious.

"Henrik, you aren't going to get anything out of her if you beat her to death. There's a reason these tactics don't work for interrogation."

"Obviously fucking her isn't working either, so what do you propose we do? If she won't talk, then I'll make her talk."

"No. Look, man. I didn't sign on for this bullshit. You're crossing a line."

"Are you fucking kidding me right now? You were all in when we handed you all that money to pay your debts. Don't whine to me now because you're a fucking pussy."

"Henrik, she's a fed. There's no covering up her missing. No making it go away. If she's not home and in bed to go to work on Monday, someone will come looking for her. Her boss is already sniffing around all her stuff."

"That's your fucking problem, Gideon. My fucking problem is cleaning up your mess. They got Red already. You still haven't given me her location. Just whose side are you on?"

Elle opens one eye, watching the two men in tuxes before her. She is purposely staying quiet as they are giving away far more information than she ever would have gotten working up the chain. She guesses Henrik is the ringleader of this whole mess, hiding behind the Kleinfeld money. It makes sense to her. Gideon is like a knife in the back. She bought him hook, line, and sinker. But she's not about to give up Joe. She doesn't care how much they beat her. Even if they kill her, Joe and Frank will solve the case. They are too close not to.

The two men begin to struggle physically with each other. She cannot make out exactly what is going on as the room is dark, or her vision is messed up. What the hell did they give her? Then it's blindingly bright as the lights are flipped on.

"Boys? What is going on in here?"

She knows that voice. "Please. Mr. Kleinfeld. Help." She gets out before she feels another fist to her gut.

Atticus's eyes narrow as he looks from his son to Gideon, then to the figure in the chair. When she turns her head in his direction, their eyes meet and he sees clearly that it is Noelle Harris strapped to the chair, in her undergarments, and has been beaten. His eyes narrow at the two young men.

"You two, my office. Now." Atticus then steps out of the doorway, disappearing down the hall.

Elle's brow furrows as the two men quickly follow him, one flipping the light back off and leaving her in the dark. She looks down at her wrists and try as she might, she cannot get any purchase. She tries to lean down to bite at the tape and is hunched over when a figure enters the room. The cloth comes over Elle's face and she goes into training mode. She doesn't gasp, or gulp for a deep breath. She stops breathing in an effort to avoid being knocked out.

In the end she has to gasp for air and the chloroform does its job.

In Atticus's office, the three men are silent. Gideon and Henrik are tussled looking, with Henrik having a bit of blood on him. Atticus, who is in a suit, not a tux, sits in his chair and rests his hands on his desk. "Care to explain to me why you have a federal agent tied to a chair in my home, Henrik?"

Gideon watches as his childhood friend crumples under the stern gaze of his father. Henrik does everything to impress his father, even in trying to make this case go away. Gideon now regrets telling Henrik of the wrinkle with the informant and interjects. "It's my fault, sir. Agent Harris knows the name of the man on the inside. He apparently is still active, and she is withholding the information from the case files. Henrik was trying to help me."

Atticus looks from his son to Gideon. He's a good kid and will make a hell of a prosecutor. He can't blame the boy for trying to defend his friend. It's an honorable trait to have, but both boys have made this difficult and now Atticus is going to have to kill one of his closest friends' child. The question is, does he kill Wolfe, or Harris? He drums his fingers against his desk. His guard has already taken Miss Harris to her accommodations until he can decide. He takes a deep breath and cuts his look back to his son, his greatest disappointment.

"The informant is Elijah Wolfe. He is going by the name Thatcher."

"What? Tomlin's new guy? The one he stole from Miles? We should go take care of that fuck right now." Henrik's agitation is high, and it makes Gideon wonder if he is dipping into something to amp him up like this.

"You will do no such thing. You two have done enough. Now. You will go home and pretend like this evening did not happen. You will go to work like normal, and you will not utter one word about Noelle Harris, or Elijah Wolfe, is that understood?"

"Yes, sir," Gideon replies, eager to be out of this house.

After much reluctance, and defeat, "Yes, father." Henrik's shoulders sag.

"Good. Now get out of my office."

# CHAPTER THIRTY-TWO

*Twas the Night Before Christmas*

*December 24, 1986*

My alarm goes off at six in the morning. I cannot wait for today. Maman and Tristan make the best breakfast. I shower, shave, comb my hair back, and put on a nice shirt with slacks. While I know it's just my family, we are expected to look nice today. We will go to midnight services, and it's a tradition at this point. I'm excited. I have not seen my family, most of them, for a hot minute. I'm particularly excited to see Hope-Marie and her two kids. I can't believe my kid sister has two kids now.

I slip on my coat and step out the door, locking it from the outside to make sure it is secure when I catch a glimpse of the Lincoln parked at the end of the street. My entire mood sours. That Lincoln doesn't belong here, and after the shit with Miles, I'm not discounting anything out of the ordinary. It would look weird if I just went back inside. They would know I've made them. With a scowl on my face, I make my way to the shit brown sedan.

When I pull out of the parking lot and head down the street, I notice the Lincoln follows. It confirms who they are here for, and that pisses me off even more. I was really looking forward to Maman's waffles, some French toast, perfectly scrambled eggs, juicy sausage, and bacon both juicy and crispy. But I'm not about to take these fucks right to my family. Especially not if they don't know who I am. With a grumble, I pull into the run-down diner a few blocks from my apartment.

I never go here, so I am not too worried about being recognized, but it's not going to be what I wanted for today. Once inside, I sit with a huff. There is a pretty little thing waiting tables today. She must be the only one with nowhere to go.

"What can I get ya?" Her voice is sweet, and she's smiling at me more than a friendly hello.

"Pancakes, eggs, scrambled with cheese, sausage, water, and coffee," I rattle off like a drill sergeant.

"You want any gravy? Or biscuits?"

"Sure. Why not." I hand her the menu and she saunters off. My eyes take in the shapely bottom she has and long legs. If I have to suffer alone today, at least I can enjoy the view, right? I lean back in the booth and give a casual glance outside. That Lincoln is parked down the street, but is definitely there for me. It brings the scowl back to my face.

The food arrives a few minutes later and I get to eating. Nothing here tastes good. It's not bad, but I was not in the mood for diner food.

"Shouldn't you be brimmin' with cheer? It bein' Christmas Eve and all."

"Bah humbug," I retort.

She laughs and leans against the booth opposite me. "What's got you all down and out?"

"My girl."

"So, get a new girl." She winks at me and is called away before I can reply.

I grin at her answer. She's easy on the eyes and is definitely sending the vibe of being into me. She takes a few minutes to come back around and clean up my dishes. She fills my coffee up with the tar they call coffee and I sit there, quietly stewing in my lack of getting to celebrate Christmas. I've left a couple of messages for Agent Harris, but it's probably better we keep missing each other. If I wanted to do anything I was going to need to lose these schmucks. I drop a fifty on the table and snatch up the napkin with her number on it before I head home.

I'm not home even five minutes when the phone rings.

"Hello," I say.

"Joooooooooooooooe!" Double Trouble whine in unison into the phone. I laugh. The twins are my youngest siblings and Double Trouble does not even begin to cover how much of a handful they are. Too smart for their own good. "You're in trouble!" They both giggle.

"Oh? That so? With who?"

"Maman," Jocelyn says.

"Papa," Cosette says at the same time.

"Hope-Marie," both say.

I laugh and rub my hand over my face. "I'm not coming today. Tell everyone I'm sorry."

"But Joooooooooooe," they whine.

"I can't. I have to work."

"HOPE-MARIE!" I hold the phone away from my ear as they shout for her. Great. Not what I need right now. I should hang up. "Joe says he won't come over for Christmas and that he hates your face!"

"Hey now! I never once said anything about faces."

"And that your baby's ugly!"

"Stop making shit up! I said the baby was wrinkly, not ugly!"

"And that you have wrinkles!"

"Really, Joe? Wrinkles?" The sweet voice of Hope-Marie comes on the line, replacing the twins. She is laughing, so I figure she knows the truth.

"Well, the picture you sent was right after she was born."

"What's this bullshit about you not coming for Christmas?"

"I can't. I'm working."

"You can take the day off for family."

"No. I can't. Listen-."

"No, you listen. I didn't fucking fly across country with a three-year-old and a one-year-old so you could fucking jack off in your apartment. Get your ass over here now."

"Hope-Marie," I sigh her name, frustrated. I can tell her anger isn't really directed at me. It's likely at the lack of sleep she is getting, and the stress of traveling. She has been having a hell of a time with her new club in New York.

"Don't Hope-Marie me. You are being a dick and I'm not having it. You have fifteen minutes before I come over there and get you."

"No! Fuck! Listen to me. You can't fucking come over here right now. I'm fucking working," I growl back at her. "And if you show up here, you're not going to fucking like it."

"Don't fucking threaten me. You know what? No. Nuh-uh. You aren't weaseling out of family time because you were out late banging some chick, or who knows what else. DAAAAD!"

I pull the receiver away from my ear again and growl. Now she has me all riled up and I can't even defend myself.

"Why are we shouting across the house?" I hear my father's voice calmly come through the receiver. He answers from another phone, probably in his office.

"Joe's being a jerk and trying to weasel out of Christmas."

"Hang up the phone, Hope-Marie."

My father waits until he hears the receiver click. "Elijah, want to tell me what is going on?"

"I would love to, pop. But I can't. And it's not that I don't want to come over, it's that I can't. I'm working a case and… It would put the family in danger."

I hear the heavy sigh on the other end. "You better damn well show up when you can. You will eat your mother's breakfast when you get here, and you will exchange gifts with the family. Until then, keep yourself safe."

"I will, pop. I'll be there as soon as I can."

"Love you, boy. Awoo."

"Awoo, pop." I hang up after that and sulk. This is not how I wanted to spend Christmas Eve at all.

The hours tick by slower than paint drying. I finally give up and head to the location Tomlin gave me about an hour early. After all, there are pretty girls and booze there. If I am going to have to suffer the holidays alone, might as well get some free booze. The place is packed. Anyone, who is anyone is here. The first person I notice is the police commissioner who is having a laugh with the deputy mayor.

I order a stiffer drink, only to set my gaze upon the fire Marshall. Fuck me, is everyone in on this? What really makes me tuck my nose into my drink is Elle's father, not fifteen feet away from me, shooting craps. I know Elle isn't all that close with her family, but this is going to tear her up. I hope to God her brother isn't here, or I'm done for.

I take my drink and quickly make my way to the locker room. So much for enjoying the atmosphere. Tomlin and my coach soon appear and are in high spirits. "You're in luck tonight. Boss man wants this to be a real humdinger. Says he's got quite the opponent for you. Opening bets are starting at fifty large."

"Fifty? Fuck. I ain't got that."

"Don't worry, kid. At big fights like this, they always give you a gimme. Besides, you're favored to lose at about ten to one."

"Lose. Why are you assholes always assuming I'm gonna lose?"

"It's cause you're scrawny," my coach chimes in.

"I'm not fuckin' scrawny. Did you not see what I did to the other guy?"

"Yeah. I did. Because you're scrawny and scrappy. Now quit your bitchin' and get ready. Show starts in thirty minutes."

I'm left to my own devices then. It affords me a few minutes to get into comfy clothes, and down the last of my drink. I can hear the roar in the arena already. It's far more packed than it was on Saturday. I would like to say I wasn't worried, but I have no idea who I am facing, and they could be a faster version of the guy I took down at The Pit.

The time comes and a cute little button of a woman dressed in hardly anything escorts me to the ring. I step out into the arena to a mix of cheers and jeers. So, I play it up and flex a little as I move around. Until I see Atticus grinning at me like a Cheshire cat. I lower my fists and make my way to my corner to wait.

He stands, raising his hands to silence the crowd. "Ladies and Gentlemen. I hope you are having a very merry Christmas. Tonight, you are getting an early present. I know you have been asking for this for months. But the opportunity has never truly presented itself until tonight."

I frown as the crowd ramps up with a mix of gasp and cheers. It is obvious this has been going on for some time. I get that horrible feeling in the pit of my stomach that I'm about to do something I really don't want to.

"Tonight. We are going to have a true Roman experience. You all know and love our up and coming, Thatcher. His prowess has even turned the mighty bull's head." I watch as Atticus works the crowd like Harold Hill singing about pool halls. "But prowess, can also get the mighty hunter in significant trouble. So, in the other corner," he waves his hand in a grand gesture. "I present to you, the jilted lover."

There is an audible silence in the room as every head turns to look at the opposite end of the ring. My eyes widen and fury fills me as I see her stumbling from being shoved into the ring. Her hair is matted, her face brown and purple, mixed with dried blood. She is holding her rib cage, and she is in nothing more than black lace undergarments, with torn stockings from what I can only imagine was duct tape. She stands tall though, not showing fear, until her eyes lock on mine across the ring.

That is when I realize what Atticus meant by Roman experience. He intends for me to kill Elle Harris.

## CHAPTER THIRTY-THREE
*Ava Maria*

Standing like a Roman emperor in his box, Atticus continues to spew idiocy to the crowd, and they eat it up like candy. All I can do is watch as Elle strides forward to meet me in the center of the ring. Up close, I can see someone has done more damage than I originally thought. I need to stall until Frank got here. I knew something wasn't right when she didn't even bother to return my calls and we were this close to catching the big fish. Then Frank called me when he got my present from the county sheriff. So, I told him what I knew about tonight. Told him to not be late as the fights don't last long, and here we are.

A quick scan of the crowd tells me Frank's late. Leave it to the feds to be standing around, holding their dicks when I need them. My gaze settles upon Elle again and I call an audible. There is no way in hell I could tell her the plan. I do the next best thing. I slap her.

The first expression I get from her is pain, as I didn't even think about where I was hitting her, and it lands right on the nasty bruise across her swollen cheek. This turns to shock, as I can guess she thought I would never raise a hand to a woman.

Or that I somehow would be the big damn hero and try to weasel my way out of this fight. If I could have a Christmas wish right now, it would be that the two of us are not standing in this damn ring. Then rage is the final look I get.

"What the fuck, Wolfe?" spouts out of her mouth.

"What? That's how you feds fight, right? Like the little bitches you are."

I did not expect that to work, but the left hook I take to the jaw tells me I pushed the right button, at least. I dance back and she pursues. Oh, that fire in her eyes. Shame there's a bunch of spectators, because that fire is hot. "Come on, princess, that all you got? Show me what you're made of."

I hope we live for me to regret the words that just came out of my mouth. I see the mix of hurt and rage in her eyes as I take the road she battles every day. But hot damn, if I thought Red was fast, Elle's strong too. She isn't play fighting and did not pick up any kind of hint I put down. Her punches come hard and fast. I can barely dance around her and block, much less take up a proper offense. The only thing keeping her at bay, as far as I can tell, is someone has already worked her over pretty well.

Note to self, do not pick a fight when she is fully healed.

"Awe, cupcake. Your little love taps, just make me want to keep this up all night." I then blow kisses at her. Or at least try to between the fury of fists flying at my face. But I see it then, the twinkle in her eye as she connects the dots. I am positive she tries to hit me even harder.

"What the fuck, Harris?" I growl when she almost gets my balls and I turn fast enough her knee connects with my thigh instead. I throw her to the ground to buy me some breathing room and quickly step back.

She springs up like a fucking weeble-wobble, smirks, and just like those damn toys I find her fist in my face. I can't look around for fear she'll cock me hard enough to knock my ass out. Which would completely defeat the purpose of staying alive until Frank gets here.

*Fuck, where is he?*

I land two blows to her rib cage, and it sends her to her knees. The guilt that fills me makes me want to rush to her and hold her, but if I do that, the jig is up. So, I take the moment to scan the crowd again, hoping beyond hope that I see anything that resembles a raid happening. So far, I am only greeted with cheering spectators out for blood. I am beginning to suspect that Frank might be in on this bullshit and one, or both of us, is going to die tonight.

*Come on Joe. What's the plan B? You gotta have a Plan B.*

In my budding panic, I lose focus on Elle. I have to give her props for her ability to find an opening and take it. Her right fist connects with my lower rib, followed by the swift one, two combo, intending to lay my ass out. Only, my instinct and reflexes kick in and I pivot around to deflect her blow with my right arm, as my left fist lashes into her jaw.

Time slows to a crawl as I watch my fist connect with that perfect jaw. Then I swear I can hear the clack of her teeth and I watch in horror as her eyes roll into the back of her head. Like Popeye without spinach, I watch her spin and crumple to the ground, knocked clean out.

"No," I bark, fear and panic lacing my voice. "Elle, no no no." I drop to my knees, cradling her to me. I lightly tap her cheek. "Come on, baby. Wake up. Wake up. Open your eyes. Fight's not done yet." That budding panic blooms into a full wildflower of fear as I hear Atticus Kleinfeld call from his box.

"Actually, my dear Mr. Wolfe, the fight *is* over." I look up to see him standing, that Cheshire grin on his face again. He holds out his hand with his thumb to the side.

"And you, my lovely friends. Now must decide. Does the jilted lover live?" He turns his thumb up. "Or does she die?" He turns his thumb down.

My eyes dart, looking for any way out of this mess. Be it a guard with a weapon, or a clear path I could just pick her up and run. I scoop her up into my arms and shift my weight to allow me to bolt for an exit, if this goes horribly. I am going to fucking kill Frank if I live through this. I watch in horror as one by one; the blood thirsty sycophants raise their hands and shove their thumbs to the floor.

"This can't be happening," I huff. The deputy mayor, thumbs down. The fucking chief of police, thumbs down. I scan the crowd and literally the only thumbs up I can see is the one man staring at the woman in my arms with the same love and compassion I am feeling, her father. Our eyes lock for the briefest of moments and I could feel that silent plea asking me to save her.

My gaze is drawn back to Atticus as once more, he hushes the crowd to speak. "Your votes have been cast, my dear friends." His grin never falters as he looks down at the two of us. I watch as he holds his hand out, thumb to the side. I count the heartbeats, waiting in terror for his final verdict. The roar of the crowd chanting, "Thumbs down" rings in my ears. I pull her closer to me, and I stand, turning her to Kleinfeld, clutching her to my chest.

"We gave you your damn fight. We've entertained your people. Made you your money. There's no need for more bloodshed."

"That, my dear Mr. Wolfe, is where you are wrong. For you see, to ensure your loyalty, I must act."

"Ensure my loyalty? What the fuck are you talking about? This is a person's life. Not some gambling chit, you fucking prick."

"Exactly. Which is why this must happen. You will finish this fight as I rule, or you both die."

I then take a moment to scan all the exits and guards again. Where there might have been a chance before, there is none now. The guards are blocking the exits, and their weapons are drawn.

"Fine! If it's fucking blood you want. Take mine. Let her go."

"That is not how this works, Mr. Wolfe. You are the victor. You are to be celebrated. And, what kind of host would I be if I betrayed the judgment of the people. They have already spoken. My hands are tied." He brings his other hand to his chest, as if he is being empathetic with our plight in ordering Elle's death.

"We both know that's bullshit, Kleinfeld."

I watch as his grin turns feral, and his thumb turns to the floor.

# CHAPTER THIRTY-FOUR
## On The Twelfth Day of Christmas

"Wolfe, please stop shaking me." Her voice is graveled and thick from sleep, but it's the sweetest sound I have ever heard.

"Welcome back to the land of the living," I tease.

"Fuck you, did I win?"

"Nope. But you're alive."

"Hrmph," she pouts.

"Don't hrmph me. That mother-fucker voted to kill you."

"I never did like the Kleinfelds," she retorts with a smile. She opens her eyes then and I watch her take in exactly where we are at. "Why the fuck are we in a hospital?"

"We're here because Frank's not dirty. That one is a keeper." I laugh as she groans and rolls her eyes.

"I'm not fucking Frank. He's married."

"Never once did I say to fuck Frank. Why would you fuck Frank?" I get defensive and then I see her grin. I can't decide if I want to strangle her or kiss her.

"What happened?"

"I think I can explain that, Agent Harris," as Frank comes walking into the room with her father.

"What's he doing here?" Elle grumbles like a petulant teenager caught playing hooky.

"Consider it a favor for an old friend," Frank says and gives me a nod to get up.

I furrow my brow, not putting together what's going on yet, either. My hackles are up seeing as I saw this rich prick at the fight last night.

"Daddy, what does he mean a favor?"

I snap my head around to look at Elle. She never talks that girly talk. If I didn't know any better, I would have described her as a scared victim and not the magnificent, foul-mouthed, dirty woman I know.

Mr. Harris sighs and lifts his hands enough to allow the cuffs under his suit jacket to rattle. As I look at Elle, I can tell we have the same expression on our faces.

"Come on, Wolfe, I have a few questions for you. Let's give them a minute."

I nod my head and give her foot a light shake as I follow Frank out, staring daggers at her father. At least that fucker didn't vote for her death.

The door closes behind me, and I cross my arms at Frank. "What the fuck? He's one of them."

"Cool your jets, kid. Yes, he is, and he has sung like the caged bird he is. Only made one demand of us. That we don't fire his kid. Admirable, but stupid. I'm not about to lose my best agent."

"So, he's going to prison?"

"Nah, no doubt Gideon'll work him some deal. They gave that redhead just about everything she asked for." Frank shrugs. "Turns out, when your rich country club buddy decides to murder your only daughter, you grow a conscience."

"Who would've thought?" Frank looks bemused at my dead-pan delivery.

I can see through the window of the door that Elle's not happy with whatever her father is saying to her. She even turns away when he tries to hug her. "That doesn't look like it's going well." I motion into the room. "Probably should save him before she gets violent."

"You think she would hit him?"

"She hit me."

"Yah, but you were fuckin' other women and she's got a thing for you."

"And when does her personal life become your problem?"

"Became my problem when she broke the fucking rules for you, Wolfe."

"Technically, if you feds hadn't kicked me off the case to begin with, she wouldn't have had to do that. So, if it's anybody's fault, it's yours, Frank."

"Uh-huh. Keep tellin' yourself that, kid," as Frank eases open the door. "Come on, time to go get your golden ticket from Gideon."

The first thing I notice is Elle goes ramrod straight and her knuckles turn white gripping the sheet. "You didn't arrest Gideon? What about Henrik?" She growls.

This makes Frank stop and turn to look between us. "What do you mean arrest Gideon? He's been helping all night with the round-up."

"Gideon's the fuck that kidnapped me. He spiked my drink. Then that pussy fuck stood there while Henrik Kleinfeld gave me a once-over, trying to get Joe's name. Only reason I got out of that damn chair is Daddy came home, and then he threw me in the ring with Joe. You might wanna rethink who's issuin' those golden tickets."

Frank furrows his brow. "I think I know a few Oompa Loompas I can call. I'll let you know how it turns out."

I watch as Elle relaxes and nods. She must trust Frank. I trust him too,now that we're out of the fight ring. Frank leads her father out of the room, leaving the two of us alone. The room falls quiet, and guilt fills me. Had I tried to get in touch with Elle after the fight on Saturday, I would have known she was missing. Fuck. I spent the week running around saving Meg, and Elle was taking a beat-down for me. She interrupts the silence by yanking out her IV.

"Whoa. Hey. What are you doing? You have at least two broken ribs, a concussion, and an untold number of other injuries. Doc said morphine drip would do you good, and you needed a few days to rest."

"I'm going the fuck home, Wolfe." She looks upset, and I can put together she means she's going to her apartment.

"Fine. Fine. The docs aren't going to let you out of here. It's not safe for you to be alone, Elle."

"I'm fine!" She snaps at me, and I watch as she stands. Then she sways like a reef on the wind before she sits roughly back on the bed.

"You're fuckin' insane if you think you're fine. Now, only way you're gettin' out of here is if I jail break you. So, if we're doing this, I'll run interference on Nurse Ratched while you slip out."

"I don't have any clothes," she chuckles. "Maybe we should start with scrubs." I watch her reach up and kill the little monitors, so they don't go off when she pulls the sensors off. I don't even want to know how she knows to do all that. I duck out of the room and make my way down the hall to where they keep the fresh linens, stealing some scrubs for her. By the time I get back, she is standing, albeit still swaying, but standing. I hand her the scrubs and watch out the door as she gets dressed. I know better than to argue with her. The woman's hard-headed enough when she's sober and at this moment she's running on morphine and daddy issues. I would have a better chance of arguing with a ballistic cruise missile than Elle Harris.

"I don't think I can walk on my own," she giggles.

"Well, it'll look a little awkward if I carry you. They'll catch us if I roll you out in a chair."

"I just need something to steady me, asshole."

I flash a grin, because there's my girl. "Fair enough. You ready?"

"Awoo," she slurs out.

I chuckle. "Close enough."

"Wait. That's not right."

"Awoo," I say with another chuckle. She comes to me, and I dump my coat around her shoulders. "Keep up," I grin.

"Wait… Wolfe-," but she stumbles along with me.

I'm pretty sure every single nurse gave us a cursory glance, then decided it was not worth the fight, especially on Christmas morning. We get out the door, uninterrupted.

"Holy fuck, it's cold," she gasps, and I look down to see her bare feet touching the ground.

Being the gentleman I am, I sweep her up into my arms like she's my blushing bride and make a break for the car. She leans in and giggles against my chest as she curls her toes to keep them warm. I get her settled into the passenger side of the shit-brown sedan. Boy, will I be glad to be rid of this car.

One upside is the heater works, and it's about the only thing that works, at raging inferno high. I'm sweating like a pig in no time flat, and she's curled up, snuggled into my jacket like it's a Christmas quilt wrapped around her.

A few minutes later she cracks open her eyes. "Hey, this isn't the way to my place."

"You're right. It isn't."

"I'm getting really fucking tired of being kidnapped."

"I think this one will be significantly more pleasant than the last time," as I turn the car onto the gravel road with a single mailbox at the entrance.

"Where are we?" She blinks, and she sits up more.

I just grin in response. She'll recognize it soon enough. I remember playing basketball with Skip while she and Hope-Marie giggled on the porch. I follow the curve and the little grove of trees give way to my parents' sprawling mansion. It really isn't that big, but they did have to accommodate twelve children and their families.

"Oh, fuck no. Nuh-uh. I'm not going in there."

"And I'm not leaving you alone for Christmas. So, either I miss the big family Christmas to babysit your ass. Or you get that fucking chip off your shoulder and enjoy Tristan's waffles."

"What about his figgy pudding?"

I grin, "Already requested, and it's for dessert."

"You have dessert after breakfast?"

I laugh because I know it's the morphine making her brain slow. "After dinner, Harris. Before we go to church."

"Church?" she whines.

"I'm one of the heathens that likes to skip it. You won't have to worry about that part."

"Fine. Okay. But really, I just want to go to sleep. I'll find a guest room and let you have your family Christmas."

"Well... That might be a little more difficult than you think," as I put the car into park. I see the identical silhouettes of Double Trouble at the door. The twins burst through and bumrush the car.

"JOOOOOOOEE!" they shriek in unison, and I see several lights flick on in the house.

If looks could kill, the death stare coming from Elle would have put me six feet under already.

# CHAPTER THIRTY-FIVE
*Have Yourself a Merry Little Christmas*

I try not to laugh as Jocelyn and Cosette stop dead in their tracks. They look at me. Look at Elle. Look at each other. My expression slowly goes from humor, to concern, to suspicion, to oh fuck no, as the two of them bolt back for the house, shouting at the top of their lungs. "AND HE BROUGHT A GIRL!" If the whole house wasn't awake before, they are now. Elle laughs like a mad-woman and it's infectious, causing me to laugh too.

"Well, no turning back now."

"We could still make a run for it. I have pop-tarts."

"But then I don't get figgy pudding."

"I'm sure Meg could fig your pudding for you," she is still laughing when she says it.

"While you are absolutely right, Meg could fig my pudding. She went home for Christmas."

"So, your place is quiet?" Elle perks up.

It's then I see a rather disgruntled and disheveled woman appear on the porch with a toddler in arm and the other hand on her hip.

"I'll trade you peace and quiet with time with a toddler."

"Two broken ribs," Elle replies in a deadpan.

"Come on, I'll carry you in, princess."

I'm pretty sure she would have decked me had I not gotten out of the car. I come around and scoop her out of the passenger seat to begin the death march to the front door. Hope-Marie is standing there like the fearsome matriarch she is, and I can't help but grin at her.

"Good to see you too, sis. You know, babies have definitely helped your figure," I chirp as I breeze by her, carrying Elle inside.

"Elijah Joseph Wolfe," I hear the shrill, angry voice of Maman. "Did you get married and not tell anyone?"

"We're not married, Ma. She just needs shoes."

"Hi. Mrs. Wolfe," Elle chirps and giggles. "He jail-broke me."

"He vhat?" Maman narrows her eyes.

"She's in scrubs, Maman. He snuck her out of the hospital. Why are you stealing women... Wait, is that Elle Harris?"

"YUP!" Elle adds, full of fake cheer. "And I really would like a bed. He is making my ribs hurt."

"Give me her," Hope-Marie snaps at me.

"Wait. You can't carry —," as my sister pretty much forces Elle out of my arms while replacing her with the balling one-year-old who wants mama only. "What... No. How am I? How do you make it stop? Shh shh. It's alright. Mommy will be right back." I try to soothe the ball of fluffy pajamas and curls in my arms. I watch in horror as my sister and Elle disappear, abandoning the miniature human in my arms. This causing her to crank it to eleven in the demands to be returned to her mother.

"Hey now," I say softer to the little one, "let's see what we got here," as I move to the cookie jar, still holding the little girl whose fingers are outstretched in the direction Mommy went, belting for all to hear this disagreement in the turn of events.

"Helena!" Maman's voice cuts across the crying. It even makes me stand up straight, as it does all of us in the room. "Zhat is enough. Say hello to your uncle. He needs lots of hugs. He missed special presents."

There is a momentary pause in the screaming, as Maman's voice startled the child. But it is a short-lived reprieve as she contemplates the words coming from Maman. Then I see it. Her mouth opens wide, and the wailing banshee cry erupts like a volcano as she becomes an expert contortionist in my arms. I would almost rather be wrestling a greased pig over trying to keep my niece in my arms. Thankfully, Mick swoops out of nowhere and gathers her into his arms. It is like someone has turned the volume off of the show. Her little hiccups dwindle to nothing as she curls happily into Daddy.

"Thank you," I mouth to him, and he grins as I finish pilfering the cookie for myself.

In trundles sibling after sibling, their short people, and then finally Pop comes strolling in with a grin on his face. "Definitely know how to make an entrance, son. Now get in there and help your brother cook those waffles. Otherwise, there might be a mutiny if we do not get to presents soon."

I laugh, hug Pop, and duck into our massive kitchen to be put to work by my youngest brother, Tristan. When I say put to work, I mean, he has me set the table. We learned the hard way to not let me anywhere near a waffle iron. He, and Double Trouble, are bouncing about in a trifecta of golden deliciousness as they prepare breakfast for the family.

I almost drop the plate in my hand as I see Elle carefully coming down the stairs in one of Hope-Marie's dresses. She looks like an angel in that little cotton dress that flows with her. They took the time to pull her hair up and give her a little make-up to help with the bruises. Not that she needs it. It's then I hear giggling from the trifecta, and I am pretty sure there is a soft chorus of, "K-I-S-S-I-N-G," floating around.

"Want to hear all the details?"

"Ew! Joe, you're a pervert."

"Hope-Marie! Stop teaching them words."

"Hey man, if the shoe fits, wear it. You are a pervert."

"I'm wounded," I mock pose.

"Nah. They're right. You're a pervert, Wolfe." Elle joins in and the entire kitchen erupts into laughter. Until Maman busts us.

"Zhat is inappropriate talk for Christmas. Now, you get zhat table set properly, or you know zhe consequences."

This wins another round of laughter from everyone. Then it's a well-oiled machine of sibling and grandchild moving all the food and condiments from the kitchen area to the table while the parents of infants are feeding and distracting the little ones from present time. Elle keeps trying to pick things up to help and inevitably loses it to another sibling, who is 'helping'. I can see the frustrated look on her face, so I dance in before she can explode. "Your seat's over here, by me."

I gently guide her to sit down. "You're a guest. You're not allowed to help." I wink at her. "What do you want to drink?"

"Whiskey."

"No can do, next."

"Tequila?"

"No Tequilla," I tease from her drunken bender. I snag the

orange juice and pour her a glass. "This is about the best I can do, for now."

"Thanks," she dead-pans, but sips it.

Breakfast is raucous and full of mirth as young Castian regales all of us with the tale of the lightsaber he found in mommy's drawer. As soon as he says, mommy's drawer, Mick and Hope-Marie change the conversation, turning on me and Elle. "So, how did you two reconnect?" Hope-Marie asks.

"An idiot crossed the river."

Elle laughs and nods in agreement.

"So, you two are still engaged, right?" Jocelyn perks up with the evilest grin I have ever seen.

"Nope. Turns out it was all a lie."

"What?!" Double Trouble whine in unison.

"Then why did we have to try on those horrible pink dresses, Mom?"

"Oh now, girls, you were so lovely in zhem."

The table erupts into laughter at the dirty looks from the twins to Maman who is grinning.

"So, you're not together?" Hope-Marie asks in a little bit of a jab.

"You know what I think?" my father interjects, saving me from twenty questions. Though I can see he has a few of his own. "I think it is time to see what Santa brought everyone."

Any further interrogation is lost in the squealing delight of a small army of children, including my siblings. We all marshal into the main living area where a massive ten-foot tree stands decorated with more shiny baubles than the Queen's jewels. Everyone takes up residence, and the designated short people pass out presents. Until they get side-tracked with their own presents and delegate the duty to the next short person in line. It's hilarious to watch them carefully plan who to give a present to in order to be the next to receive one. It goes to prove all of the Wolfe children and grandchildren are evil geniuses.

I'm lost in the revelry of presents, which takes hours by the way, until I realize Elle hasn't said a word for some time. I look up and I see her leaning in the doorway between the kitchen and the living room with a small frown on her face. I extract myself from the group and make my way over. "You doin' alright, Trouble?"

"Trouble?"

"With a capital T."

Then, on cue, "That rhymes with P and stands for pool!" The entire room choruses to my call. It makes Elle turn as red as the wrapping paper ribbons but laughs.

I step closer, gently placing a hand on her waist. I don't care if my family is watching me, all I can think about is keeping that smile on her face. I wanted to tell her I had been thinking a lot about us, and that I wanted us to be an *us*. But the only word that comes out of my mouth is, "Awoo?"

And I swear to God, this woman gets me. Her only reply, is the sweetest high-pitched song of, "Awoo!"

To seal the deal, I kiss her hard and hot.

\* \* \*

## Biography

J. R. Froemling was born in Indiana, the second eldest of three. She met her first husband in an online writing community. She met her second husband at a board game convention in 2015. She has a Bachelor's of Science in Information Technology from Western Governors University of Indiana. She got her start in an online writing community for Star Wars fan fiction. Over the past twenty years she has transformed that love of fan fiction into works of her own.

**Want to find out more about J. R. Froemling?**

**https://jrfwriting.com**

# Other Books By J. R. Froemling

**<u>Savannah Nights Series</u>**

    The Triple Six

**<u>The Wolfe Legacy</u>**

    Mistress Giselle - Book One of Hope-Marie

    A Devil's Hope - Book Two of Hope-Marie on Kindle Vella

**<u>Chronicles of Nodd</u>**

    Fall of Avalon - Verse One on Kindle Vella

**<u>Immortal Love Saga</u>**

    My Viking Alpha

Made in the USA
Columbia, SC
27 March 2022